WINTERBOURNE

S. A. BAKER

WINTERBOURNE
S. A. BAKER

Science Fiction and Fantasy Publications

http://scififantasypublications.com

An imprint of DAOwen Publications

Winterbourne / S. A. Baker
Edited by Douglas Owen

ISBN 978-1-928094-06-7

EISBN 978-1-92094-07-4

Jacket art: MMT Productions

10 9 8 7 6 5 4 3 2 1

To

Those who can do, those who can't, teach and those that think about doing write novels. This is dedicated to Isobel who was always excited about my writing, even when I wasn't.

WINTERBOURNE

It was cold. Colder than she thought it should be for mid-September. She could already see her breath in the air most nights, and the jacket she ordered out of the fall catalogue was neither warm enough, nor designed for a woman well into her ninth month of pregnancy. Practicality, she decided, was never one of her strongest suits. At 23 she had known the man whose child she now carried for a grand total of seven and a half hours.

The young woman went to the house warming party with no designs apart from getting drunk and not falling in love. When she saw the tallish man sitting on the sofa watching television, she reasoned half a plan was better than none at all. Within an hour of her arrival, she had drunk enough to talk to him. After two hours she bordered on sloppy, hanging on his every word, and at three hours, she unbuttoned his shirt in a taxi on the way back to her apartment.

There had been too many partners, she thought, most of them anonymous faces and willing bodies. She felt rootless and unapologetic and her life became a circle of self-deprecation, self-medication, and self-degradation. Her life headed down a tunnel she couldn't see the other side of and didn't care if she made it back to the light unscathed or not. She pushed him down on to her bed and threw herself on top of him; she kissed him hard and deep and forgot for a moment how ashamed she would feel about herself in the morning.

The sunlight poured across her face through windows she swore she covered with curtains the night before. Her brain attempted to open an eye but the thunder inside her skull made it nearly impossible. The young woman managed to get one almost half open and noticed him standing in front of the window, naked from the waist and looking at her. Not exactly staring but fixed on her just the same. He was beautiful; fit but not too muscular with a shock of dark hair that framed his face perfectly. But it was his eyes, those blue eyes that she could see so clearly even through the whisky cowl that covered her vision. She saw her whole life inside his crystal blue gaze. He reached for his shirt and let out a sigh full of satisfaction.

"Best time of the day," he said.

"What?" she croaked.

"I was saying this is the best time of the day, first thing in the morning." His voice had a lyrical, soulful sound to it. Nondescript and slightly British sounding, she would normally have loathed it but it served to endear him to her.

"I don't expect I'll be seeing you again," she said.

"There are no chance meetings," he said. "Everyone who comes into your life makes a hole in it that only they can fill again."

"So I ... won't see you again?" she asked, not quite getting the gist of what he meant.

"We will see each other again. I promise."

"Look," she began to speak through impossibly dry lips. "I am not in the habit of bringing home strange men."

He finished buttoning his shirt and crossed the room to where she lay in bed.

"Yes, you are," he said in a tone that left her feeling ashamed but at the same time, let her know he didn't share her shame.

She had tried to rise to meet him but the nausea dancing about in the pit of her stomach forced her back down. He bent low and kissed her forehead. She wrapped her arms around him and was surprised to find him returning the hug. She felt a warmth envelop her, like a cosy blanket and a bowl of soup from her mother. She felt a tear trickle down her face but not from sadness at his leaving; rather it was from the joy of having met him. A feeling took hold of her, like her heart might explode and leak molten sugar and she was embarrassed at herself for feeling decidedly teenaged and gooey. Still she didn't pull away from the embrace, she drew closer to it and felt the warmth radiate from every pore of him. She felt pure and innocent, she felt radiant and beautiful. She felt loved.

Time had since come and gone and there was no sign of him, but she knew there wouldn't be and, after four weeks and a lot of hand wringing, when the stick she peed on turned bright blue, she knew in a way he would be with her forever and that was all right.

At exactly 9 months, 22 hours, and 41.2 seconds, the child growing inside of her decided it was time to get out and enjoy the world. At first she thought she messed the bed in her sleep. It wouldn't have been the first time, but when the crushing spasm of a contraction pushed her knees up around her chin, she was pretty certain she wasn't drunk and that her baby was on its way out. She wondered what she should do next—should she call a cab? That might take too long and the thought of having this child in her grubby apartment was not one she relished. Sure, it was okay to live in but it was far from the sterile environment one hopes to be in when bringing something completely defenseless and exposed into the world. She could call an ambulance, but that seemed like too much of a bother and the fire department would likely turn up first. What if there was a really attractive fireman, the kind with a square chin and strong white teeth who smiled all the time and laughed at all of her jokes, no matter how bad they were. What if he saw her as really quite pretty until the whole birthing thing kicked into high gear and she began to look like a grimacing, nightmarish blob of flesh, wailing and grunting like a well-stuck boar? What if she just drove herself to the damned hospital and hoped she had enough change to park for the duration?

The contractions seemed to calm a little as she unlocked the door of her car. She supposed the baby liked the idea of arriving to the hospital on its own terms—she did too. When her water broke and woke her, she got out of bed and put on her shoes and the uncomfortable fall jacket. Now the coldness of the night air against her wet sweat pants left her wishing she had changed her clothes. She thought of going back in the apartment to clean up and put on something drier and warmer but the baby didn't like this kind of practical thinking and sent her a contraction that nearly dropped her to her knees.

"All right, all right," she said out loud. "We're going."

She pulled out of the parking lot and headed west, she had practiced this route endlessly, figuring she would drive herself or at the very least, tell the cab driver the fastest way to get there. Her favourite song came on the radio and she sang along as she pulled up to a red light.

"I'm taking a ride with my best friend," she sang. "Ungh!" A contraction hit, the baby liked the song too.

The light turned and she drove on toward the hospital.

"I hope he never lets me down again, ungh!" she gasped. "C'mon! It's just a little further, not yet!"

She stopped at the light two blocks from the hospital and worried she wouldn't make it that far. The vision of the fireman seeing her make horrible birthing faces spurred her on and so she turned up the radio and sang louder.

"He knows where he's taking me!"

The contraction that came was so intense she had to brace herself against the passenger seat to keep from curling up in a ball and sobbing. In doing so, she knocked her purse to the floor. Good sense would have told her to let it fall, but instinct told her that something was falling and she needed to retrieve it. Instinct is sometimes a vicious and powerful thing. Her arm shot downward, toward the falling bag, before her brain had time to realize what she was doing. The radio blared and in an instant, she resumed her role in a chain reaction that began the night she met the man at the party.

"Taking me where I want to be..."

Her head dipped below the dashboard for a split second. That was all it took.

Time seemed to slow and in the hours it took for her look back up over the dashboard, the navy blue Chevy Impala crossed the center line and bore down on her.

"Promises me I'm as safe as houses, as long as I remember who's wearing the trousers."

Instinct took hold again and the wave of the contraction that washed over her made her think of the child before the car she drove. She grasped her belly with both hands and let go of the steering wheel. The young woman caught a glimpse of the Impala driver's face as the two cars became one. It was him.

"Never want to come down."

The two cars embraced and she thought, for a moment, that it was much quieter than she imagined it would be. A bit of a thud and a jostle and in a moment she would be exchanging pleasantries and insurance information with him and discussing the best possible way to raise their child. A heartbeat passed and she felt the rough music of the window exploding beside her and spray her face with a hundred angry hornets.

"I'm taking a ride with my best friend."

She felt a tightness in her chest and found it hard to breathe. Her thoughts flashed to the baby and she started to panic but felt slightly calmer when it kicked. She wanted to sit up but couldn't. She wanted to scream for help but didn't have the energy. She opened her eyes and there he was, standing over her, holding her in the deepest blue half-stare once more and she tried to rise and meet him but the steering column forced her back down. He bent low and kissed her forehead.

"Everything is going to be all right," he said.

She wanted to reply, wanted to say a thousand things to him, wanted to say a single word to him, to anyone, but she couldn't. He held her hand for a moment and she thought he might have said something but she wasn't sure. She could feel his warmth in her hand and it was like sliding into a bubble bath after three or four glasses of wine.

"It's nearly time," he said.

She could feel him pull off her pyjama bottoms and wanted to tell him to stop but the wine was so good and the bath looked so warm and inviting so she put a foot in. The young woman was suddenly aware of a pressure underneath her, like an elephant pushing a grape through the back of her spine with a steam shovel. With the other foot in the water now, the pressure subsided a little.

"That's just fine," he said.

She had been worried about something, something she couldn't quite remember. Her car? Did she lock the door to her apartment when she left? Suddenly it came flooding back—the baby. She had been on her way to have a baby. Did she have the baby? How was the baby? She began to panic and tried to sit up, writhing and wriggling and trying to get away from the pain that was all over her now.

"Shhh…" he said and in the calmness of his voice, she felt herself take another sip of wine and inch a little deeper into the water.

She was in up to her waist now and keenly aware she didn't actually care about anything but getting into this tub and going to sleep.

"Nearly there," he said to her as she felt the water rise over her chest.

"Mmmm…" she purred.

She felt the warmth of the water envelop her whole body, felt the bubbles tickle her nose and fought to keep her eyes from closing.

"You did so well," he said.

She saw him as she had seen him that first morning, glowing in the new light of a new day, she saw her son in his arms wriggling and crying in the same glow. She felt the soft heat of tears rolling down her cheeks, her heart smiled and sleep took her.

CHAPTER 1

Davis Mareth sat in the lobby of Winterbourne Home and waited to be called in for his final interview with the nursing home's managing director. He recently graduated, but the youth of his education was betrayed by the care lines that etched his face and the dark circles under vibrant blue eyes. Twenty-seven - too young to look as old as he did, but having seen and known more anguish than he'd care to admit, and his face reflected it well.

"You can go in now," the receptionist said.

Winterbourne Home stood perched high atop a hill on the western most edge of the town Winterbourne. Once a state-run hospital for the mentally ill, now a place no one spoke about. If you were fortunate to secure job within its walls, you strolled along easy street for the duration of your employment, but that security came at a price. While there were many pats on the back for landing such a fine position, it was widely suspected unnatural things go on at the top of the hill, things decent folk didn't, or wouldn't, discuss in polite company. God bless if you worked behind its doors—God help if you lived behind them.

It was built in 1878 on the sprawling 350-acre estate of the town's namesake. The rear of the property bordered a dense, nearly impassable hardwood forest, and beyond that, the frigid Nyegard River rushed along below a steep, 70-foot slope. The home itself was constructed over the burnt-out ruins of the Winterbourne Estate and was intended to be the most modern 600-bed psychiatric treatment hospital in the Western world. Old man Winterbourne went mad one frigid December and burnt the place to the ground, killing himself and all of his family. It was only fitting the grounds became a place of solace for the one thing money couldn't fix.

The ominous building stood four-stories tall, constructed of red brick with dormers on all four corners of the roof and a five-story tower that jutted up through the center of the building's face like a railroad spike that hadn't quite been driven in. By 1880 it housed 2,600 patients and though no expense was spared when employing the latest techniques or the most compassionate staff, the whispers already spread through town about what really was going on up the hill. By 1900 the allegations of abuse began to surface, and by 1912 investigations into the appalling conditions and inmate bodies floating down the Nyegard River in ever-growing numbers made their way to the courts. In 1920 the doors were ordered shut for good and patients sent to other facilities.

Time and tide pass slowly and change even more so. Attempts were made, calls placed, but in the end, Winterbourne housed more than 200 residents and 100 staff until the final resident was relocated in August of 1973. Soon after its windows boarded, doors chained and the acts of unspeakable cruelty and horror whispered about and feared by a generation were covered over and forgotten.

Fifteen years later, when the town's only nursing home was destroyed by a suspicious fire, the town council squawked and balked at the thought of spending money to build a new facility. One young and inexperienced councillor suggested Winterbourne Home be renovated and turned into a state-of-the-art nursing home and he was immediately shot down.

"We can't put anyone up there," a senior councillor said. "There hasn't been anyone up there in years."

But when the young councillor asked why, no one had a satisfactory answer to give him. The building had, in recent memory, always been empty, but few could remember why. The idea was bounced around and the more it was discussed the more reasonable it began to sound. Nancy Seasons, the head of the town council and primary holder of its purse strings, smelled an opportunity, took up the idea and ran with it. Certainly the building was big enough, and with its past history as a fully equipped institution it was already halfway prepared to be a healthcare facility. It was out-dated perhaps but it wasn't out of the question, and with Nancy at the helm of the new place, how could it fail? She pushed, intimidated and rallied the support she needed until the town council finally gave in and brought it to a town meeting.

"I'll tell you why goddamned not," growled the white-haired man as he stood up. "Death himself roams the halls of that place. Anybody who goes up that hill won't come back down in anything but the back of a hearse."

"You do know how a nursing home works, yes?" Nancy Seasons barely disguised the dismissive tone in her voice. "We are all aware of the opinions you have of your former workplace and they have been duly noted."

Ezra Schneider pushed his chair back and started out of the meeting hall. He stopped, turned to the assembly and pointed directly at the town council seated on the dais.

"Mark my words," he hissed. "If you put seniors up that hill you'll wish you'd listened to me this day. That goddamned place is wrong and no good will ever come of it. Satan shit on that spot a hundred years ago and it's been poison ever since. You will all learn what it is to suffer if you don't stop this madness now."

He could feel the eyes of the room burning a hole through the middle of his back and the tension of forcibly restrained laughter would have made a lesser man tuck tail and run. Unabated, he met as many eyes as possible and glowered at them all before slowly making his way to the doors.

"Thank you again, Ezra."

Nancy Seasons eyed the rest of the town council with a sneer—the kind of look that only comes from people who feel a profound sense of superiority and entitlement as they evict grandmothers and tell children Santa Claus is really their parents.

"No further objections, then?" Nancy asked. She began to raise her gavel as a hand slowly rose from the crowd.

"Bill Watson, do you have something to say? Is it about your liquor license? If I remember, it's just about time to renew that ol' license, yes?"

The last three words fell out of her mouth in a staccato rhythm that sounded like gunshots and brought a hush over the whole room. The hand lowered quickly and Nancy Season's gavel fell.

Ezra Schneider walked the 13 steps out of the town council building and on to the street.

"Those assholes wouldn't know danger if came up and poked them in the eye with a bastarding station wagon," Ezra grumbled. He walked to the corner of the town's main intersection and waited for the traffic to stop.

That had been 10 years ago, and as far as anyone knew nothing evil, depraved or even out of the ordinary happened up at Winterbourne Home. There were no cryptic ceremonies, no lights flashing, no burning candles and no chanting sycophants. Seniors came in family cars, taxis and city buses then left in hearses as Ezra had so ominously predicted. But it was a nursing home after all; nobody expects to leave a nursing home the way they came in. It is only well-intentioned children, in the full grips of denial, who think their parents will come out of places like Winterbourne in anything other than a shroud.

CHAPTER 2

He heard the door click as the receptionist pressed the lock release allowing him to pass through the now-open door. The director sat behind a huge, ornate antique desk dead center in a room much too small to house it. She read a small stack of papers and motioned for Davis to sit without a word to him and without looking up.

The chair sat directly in front of the desk and the smallness of the room made him feel uncomfortably close to the woman behind the desk. He found himself wondering if he's remembered to put on deodorant or brushed his teeth well enough.

"I've really been looking forward to meeting—" Davis began.

The woman raised a finger to silence him the way an unpleasant school teacher would to her unruly class, signifying she was at the end of her rope. A raised finger would be the last act of pleasantry they would see for a long time to come if they didn't settle down this very instant.

Davis fidgeted; he wanted to look at his watch but thought better of it. He reasoned that if she caught him it would set a tone for the interview he would be hard-pressed to change. And so he sat. His gaze began to wander around the room; it was sparsely decorated with various awards and certificates to demonstrate to anyone who came in just how important she was. He noticed there were no pictures, nothing to say anything of a life outside this place. No children or spouse or anything that provided a measure of her humanity. Just these bits of paper wrapped in glass that decried Nancy Seasons passed 'Basic Elder Care Module One' and Nancy Seasons showed an adequate knowledge base to obtain the position of 'Director of Care'. He glanced over at her still hunched form and felt a little sad.

She looked up and leaned back in her chair letting out a breath that seemed held for as long as Davis had been in the room. The woman took several more impossibly deep breaths and rubbed her face while getting up from her chair. She walked back and forth in what little space was left behind the massive desk and muttered with such veracity that Davis though she might have been a resident rather than the director of this home. Davis looked at his watch in spite of his conscience telling him not to. He sat, virtually silently, in this office, for 25 minutes and she had remained mute for the entirety. He was about to tell her to stuff her job when she finally blurted out,

"I don't like men."

"I'm sorry?" Davis asked not certain if he heard her correctly.

"Don't be sorry," Nancy said. "I don't like men, I don't think they have the profundity of compassion to care for the elderly the way a woman can. You are qualified, yes?"

"I, ah..." Davis began, unsure what to say next. "I assure you that my abilities are—"

"That being said…" She stopped mid-sentence and began to pace back and forth behind her desk again. It reminded Davis of a clock with a broken spring, getting a bit farther each time it attempted to click forward another minute only to stall out and wait for the mainspring to load up again.

"You can start on the night shift tonight, yes?" she asked point blank.

"Of course." Davis matched her tone in a way that surprised him.

"Good," she said. "My name is Nancy Seasons and this is not my office. I am having a new one constructed just there." She pointed toward a set of closed double doors.

"I am the director here at Winterbourne. I have a good feeling about you Mr. Mareth, but I will tell you now, if I ever hear anything dubious about you or your behaviour during your time here, I will hang you out to dry. We are clear, yes?"

"We are clear, Nancy," said Davis.

"Ms. Seasons, please," said Nancy Seasons.

Davis walked out of the office feeling as though scolded by an aunt who didn't like him very much. He felt she would have sent him packing but something, or someone, was preventing her from doing it. Whatever the reason, she gave him the job and in spite of himself, he felt pretty good about it.

Davis knew it was pointless to go home and sleep. The combination of excitement and panic about the job and what it entailed told him he would not come anywhere close to sleep in the nine and a half hours before his shift.

I'll just lie down. That way I'll at least get some rest and with a little luck, I might just fall asleep. It sounded ridiculous as it tumbled about in his mind. He returned to his apartment at 2:15 p.m. and made the decision to try and rest by 2:45 p.m. By 6:15 p.m., he just about had enough of staring at the ceiling waiting for sleep to hit him. At 7:00 p.m., he gave in and got out of bed.

He flipped on the bathroom light The fluorescent bulb flicked, fluttered and threatened to burn out altogether, just as it made a sound like a moth in a mayonnaise jar and sparked to life. Davis turned on the water for a shower and stared at himself in the mirror.

"Faaaahhhkkk!" He ran both hands through his hair. Davis looked in the mirror at the exhausted face staring back at him. It wasn't unattractive. The darkness of his hair framed his face well, even If two or three strands never managed to stay out of his face. Nor was he classically handsome, his nose was a little too crooked and his complexion was a little too pale for his liking. However the dying bulbs above the mirror cast forgiving shadows across his face that made him think he might even pass for good-looking in some circles. He caught himself looking into his own eyes. It wasn't vanity; it was a vaguely unhealthy obsession with the nearly indescribable color.

His eyes were blue. They were bluer than a summer sky after your first kiss; they were slightly bluer than a '49 Packard just off the lot and paid for in cash. So blue, they were nearly as blue as the bottom of icebergs that had formed close to the dawn of time and only the recklessly bombastic and the crazy brave had ever seen. Davis rubbed his eyes and wished they weren't so bloodshot.

"Blue and red go together, yes?" he asked the mirror then stepped into the shower.

At 9:45 p.m., Davis Mareth walked up the stairs to the entrance of Winterbourne Home and made his way through the front door. The night watchman grunted and waved him past without as much as a glance. He looked old enough to be a resident and Davis wondered if the guard looked up for anybody. The exhausted young man got the impression the guard didn't care who came in, so long as they didn't make him sign anything or ask him to look away from *Wheel of Fortune*.

Davis hurried to the broom closet that was the men's changing room and put on his uniform. He unfolded his schedule and saw that he would be working with another employee for the first night while he learned the routines of the shift and he didn't want to be late to the floor. If he risked being reported he would have to stand before Nancy Seasons and he just wasn't interested in another face to face encounter with her. It was the feeling, even though there were likely powers above her, that she could make his life very uncomfortable if she chose to and he didn't want to give her the opportunity.

"Hi, I'm Jenn," the dark haired woman said.

She was a little on the heavy side but not afraid of it. Her self-confidence made her beautiful in a very old-fashioned kind of way and Davis felt it as soon as he saw her.

"People will tell you different, but this is really the best shift in this place," she said.

"Why is that?" asked Davis.

"Because you don't have to change too many shitty diapers or deal with too many old buggers calling you nasty names and falling asleep in their goddamned oatmeal and telling you that your parents didn't love you because your belt doesn't match your eyes."

Davis stared at her for a moment and saw all the pretty drain from her face. Suddenly she looked bitter, twisted, and he wasn't sure what he should say next. She bowed her head and took a deep breath. Her head remained down for a long time, longer than Davis thought it should. She heaved another sigh that bubbled up into a crescendo of little girl laughter.

"Okay," she began. "Let's start with Mrs. Maddox."

Davis looked at Jenn as though she had sprouted horns and followed her into a darkened room. The first thing that struck him was just how small the space was. It reminded him of a prison cell in a black-and-white movie—nine by five and little else.

Not much was said, a gentle removing of clothes and a quick change of undergarments and gestures from Jenn to assure continued quiet. Davis was almost certain after his third such, nearly silent encounter, that he had absolutely no business pursuing a career in the same place as this woman.

"C'mon," Jenn said.

"I know how to change a person," Davis said. "I'm not going to learn anything about the people here just standing quietly in the background."

"I know what you can do," Jenn began. "I also know Mrs. Helm sent three people to the hospital last year with nasty infections. I hear one of them damn near lost an arm to it. Mrs. Helm doesn't like new people and she hates men. She'll lure you in by being nice and sweet and when you get close enough, she pounces like goddamned leopard. She's old, but she's fast."

Davis stood in stunned silence for an eternity before he spoke.

"Jesus Christ... are you serious? Almost lost an arm?"

"Naw, I'm just pulling your leg." A large, friendly smile crossed her face. "I tell the same story to everyone who starts here with me. Most leave after their lunch break; we'll see how long you last."

Davis stared at her for a while. She seemed suddenly very compassionate and protective, like a mother rabbit throwing herself into the fox's mouth to save her kits.

"That's not funny," Davis protested.

"Yes it is," said Jenn. "And when you've been here for a while, you'll get the joke. You may even laugh. We need to go to Ada Benson now. Watch your hands, she loves to hold hands and her hands are usually covered in shit."

They continued on and Davis, despite his earlier protests, remained silent. Partly to not startle the people they were changing and partly because he felt a little overwhelmed by everything he was taking in.

"Look, you came into this job for the same reason I did, I'm thinking. You figured you could make a decent amount of money and if you kept your head down you could avoid admitting just how fucked up your life has become because everyone around you is falling to pieces, literally. Something like that?"

"Something like that." Davis tried to disguise the embarrassment in his voice.

"I had a junkie boyfriend who knocked me around every chance he got; in spite of the fact that I was carrying his kid and I had an unhealthy habit of my own. One night I waited till he passed out and I took whatever I could grab and I didn't look back."

"Jenn, I don't know what to say," Davis began. His eyes met hers and he could see the grin that was lurking behind them, dying to spread the joke to her mouth.

"Really?" he sputtered. "Really? You suck. Do you know that? Has anyone informed you today that you suck?"

"That's the spirit," she said. "This place changes you. When I came here I figured I would be making enough money to keep my mother and me out of the poorhouse. My plan was to keep looking for something better paying and move on when I got it. I've been here for so long now I couldn't leave if I wanted to. The people here need us, need you, and you will grow to need them. You become attached to them far more than they become attached to you and when they go, when they die, a little piece of you dies with them. They are all still here and you can't leave them alone in this place, you can't leave any of them in the hands of somebody like Nancy Seasons. It isn't right."

Her voice trailed off at the end and Davis thought she might come across with another big grin, but knew in his heart she would not. She had clearly been touched by something—many somethings—and was playing them over in her mind like a movie projector. He wanted so badly to say something poignant but thought better of it.

"You have a good heart, I can see that," Jenn began after a time. "They will like you here."

"I don't think Nancy Seasons likes me very much," he said.

"Nancy Seasons is a bloated spinster who has no business being anywhere near vulnerable people," Jenn spat. "I meant the people who live here are going to like you. You will be a godsend to them."

"I don't know about that," Davis said nervously.

"I can tell about people, and I'm saying you will be great for this place and for the people in it," Jenn said.

They carried on through the night, changing people and sharing stories. Davis learned more about Jenn in the time they spent shuffling people in the half light, than he knew about people he had been with all of his life. He felt very comfortable, really, having just met her and he found himself telling the woman things that he had never told anyone. There were people that you couldn't help but unburden yourself to and Jenn was one of them. He felt like they had made a connection, not in any sexual sense but in a deep way that knew they would be in each other's lives for a long time to come, and he felt energized by it.

Some of the seniors woke as they turned and rolled them in their beds, some barely stirred. Still others were wide awake and engaged in conversations with Davis, seeming excited that somebody new had come to their floor.

He became aware that a small, silver-haired woman watched him intently throughout the night. She shuffled along 10 or so paces behind him and every time he thought she had given up and gone to bed, there she was again. A silver haired head would peer out from behind corners at him, so he just caught glimpses of her in his peripheral vision. The elderly woman carried on as though her every action was covert and clandestine, though Davis was totally aware of everything she did. So, apparently, was Jenn.

"That's Lois," she said.

"She's been following us all night?" Davis asked.

"Mostly, she's in room 107 and doesn't really sleep anymore. She usually comes out and talks, but when she saw you she must have thought something was going on. Nobody likes change around here. Change usually means losing something. Transferred to a new shift, moving on or dead, it all hurts and they don't do well with pain."

Davis could see the old woman out of the corner of his eye straining to hear what they talked about. She gave up and waved her hands in frustration in the direction of them and disappeared around the other side of the wall.

"Let's go," Jenn said.

"Where now?"

"We're done; it's time to go home."

Davis looked at the clock. Just before six in the morning. Eight hours had passed and it felt as though he just started. His first night had come and gone and he had survived despite feeling completely useless. The day staff rushed past, going about their routines as though he weren't there at all. He was tired enough that he felt like he wasn't. Davis supposed he would meet them some other time. Or maybe he wouldn't meet them at all; he didn't much care either way. He wanted to meet his bed, wanted to crawl in it and forget that he had ever done anything in his life but sleep.

"You're on your own tomorrow," Jenn said in an ominous tone.

He thought through the fog of his nearly comatose mind and in the glare of institutional lighting that she looked a little like she was floating on a cloud, or maybe lying on a freshly laundered pillow.

"I've got Lois," he said to the inviting pillow. "I'll be just fine."

"You haven't got her just yet." A look of seriousness came over Jenn's face. "But be kind to her, she knows a lot more than people around here give her credit for."

Davis stared at her, feeling as though she had just given him a warning. The seriousness was quickly replaced by a girlish laugh.

"You'll do fine: just don't try to be something you're not. I'll see you around."

CHAPTER 3

Davis walked down the steps and headed for the corner. He could get a bus to take him to the station then grab a train for the seven-mile ride home. The young man didn't own a car-he didn't like them, though he had no explanation why. It wasn't a save-the-environment, hug-a-tree thing but just the thought of being in a car made him uncomfortable and vaguely ill. As a rule he avoided them and traded the uneasiness for the wondrous odours of upstate mass transit.

Davis spied a homeless man sidling up out of the corner of his eye and glanced down to his feet, hoping not to catch the shabby man's eye. He wanted to be a bastard and be standoffish and rude like so many others, but couldn't. There was something that allowed him to see beyond the surface, almost right into people's souls and see them for what they really were. He couldn't explain it, but a simple touch and he could see a person for all they were and ever would be. Homeless people, the bungled and the botched, the wretched refuse that the world really didn't give a damn about seemed to hone in on him, no matter where he was. Davis reasoned they knew what he could do and would give them a fair shake, regardless of what they looked like. Or that he was a sucker, an easy mark and they could see him coming a mile away.

"Please," said the ragged, filthy, middle-aged man. "Please, my friend, take me. Take all of this from me."

Davis could smell booze and stale urine on the man and thought he might vomit from the smell if he got much closer.

"Please," said the man. "Please help me."

Davis reached into his pocket and came out with $17—$11 of which he would need to get home, 34 cents, and a lump of fuzzy blue lint. He thought about sticking his hand back as quickly as it came out and leaving its contents perfectly intact.

Why me? Why always me taking care of these grubby fuckers?

The vagabond reached out a foul, blackened claw of a hand and grabbed hold of Davis' arm. His attention immediately snapped to the man's face and the piercing green eyes that gave his face radiance despite the sooty countenance surrounding them. Davis felt as though he travelled at speeds beyond speed. In a heartbeat he stood beside an immaculately dressed man kissing a wife, and a little girl and walking out the door. With a flash he sat beside the well-dressed man as he threw the telephone from his desk and fell to his knees sobbing. A second after that he saw the same man pleading with his wife to stay and not take their child away from him. Davis felt himself being pulled forward, toward the bus stop, but not before a profound sadness and hopelessness surrounded this man.

He blinked and was back at the bus stop listening to the man ask him for change again

"Please," said the man sounding a bit more demanding. "Please my friend! I need to go, please!"

Davis took $5.34 out of his pocket and put it into the impossibly grimy hand as his bus pulled up.

"Do you think this will get me where I need to go?" the homeless man shouted.

"What do you want from me?" Davis shouted back.

The homeless man shouted something back to Davis, but it was made unintelligible by the chirping of the bus' air brakes as it pulled away. Davis swore he said "Meth."

"You're a sucker," Davis said and sat down in an empty seat.

CHAPTER 4

S he could feel him, he was close. His breaths were shallow and rapid, and getting faster by the minute. It wouldn't be long now. She put her face to his, looked into his eyes and could see the exquisite agony behind them. Nancy Seasons could make him suffer all night if she wanted, but she was growing bored and wanted it to be over. Still, to make him suffer a little longer, let him know just who was guiding things turned her on that much more. She slowed her pace and heard his breathing respond accordingly and leaned down to whisper in his ear.

"Now."

His breath quickened to match his pulsing and she felt he was about ready. She rose up just in time to feel the warm thick liquid hit her chest and run down over her bare breasts.

"Good," she moaned. "So good... ungh..."

She remained in that position until there was nothing left of him then rose and reached for her robe. Nancy ran a finger across her breasts and licked off the liquid that ran down them toward her navel. Frustrated by his immobility, she stood above his naked body and waited for him to open his eyes.

"That was *wonderful*," she said with as much sincerity as she could manage without going overboard and betraying her lack of sincerity. "But Mama has a busy day tomorrow so you need to go. Shower is that way and there are fresh towels under the sink."

"But I thought—" the young man began.

"You have a bright future in the mayor's office. Let's not spoil that by thinking, yes?"

Junior councillor Caleb Sutherland climbed out of bed and headed toward the bathroom. The water was already running as he opened the shower door, though he couldn't remember her getting up to turn it on. He got in and began to wash himself, grinning a victorious grin and thought about how he had her just where he wanted. His prowess in the bedroom would translate to big movement downtown. Nancy would go to bat for him now, if she wanted the pleasure of his company again that is. She stepped into the shower and his grin widened. He cupped her breast with a soapy hand and felt himself become erect.

"Don't," she snarled as though the young man had never been anywhere other than behind her in this shower, annoying the piss out of her.

He opened the curtain at the rear of the shower and slinked out, without the benefit of having rinsed the soap off. Caleb grabbed a towel from under the sink, dried and dressed himself and headed out the front door, figuring he could call a cab from the payphone at the corner.

Nancy stepped out of the shower and examined herself in the full length mirror. She was not the traditional definition of beauty, nor any definition of beauty to be honest. Rubenesque, yes she was, but her face was puffy and tired-looking most of the time and it was capped, badly, by hair whose color defied description. Her eyes were more bloodshot than anything else and she wore heavy black makeup around them that made her look as though she had been crying for hours.

She dropped her towel and stood in silence. A grin spread across her face as she looked at herself more intently. She liked what she saw—not the slightly overweight, middle-aged, sagging skin and floppy breasts that looked back from the mirror, but the raw power behind black-rimmed eyes that saw the whole affair. Nancy Seasons had power in this town and she wielded it like a scythe, swiftly, terribly and mercilessly against anyone who dared to stand in her way. It was this kind of power that brought the attractive junior counsellor to her door tonight and a promise to use the power that would bring him, and others just like him, back in a steady stream for as long as she wanted.

After she grabbed a large handful of hair gel from under the sink and slicked it through her hair, Nancy combed her hair straight back using her favourite pink comb and smiled a malignant smile at the way it hardened her appearance. The middle aged woman removed the ornate lid and stuck two fingers into a crystal bowl full of viscous black liquid. She smeared a line from one temple, across both eyes and ended at the other temple. Nancy Seasons turned out the bathroom light and spun to leave and caught a glimpse of her full form reflected in the mirror and the poisonous grin appeared again.

A single, naked bulb flickered to life as Nancy Seasons made a slow, purposeful descent into the one-roomed basement. The walls were dust covered and years of neglect left them more the color of the cinder blocks than the white paint that flaked away. In the center of the room sat an ancient man in a wheelchair. She looked into his eyes, the pale blue eyes and nearly non-existent pupils. His end was drawing near.

The old man's breaths were shallow, rapid and getting faster by the minute. It wouldn't be long now. She put her face to his, looked into the milky, nearly sightless eyes and she could see the exquisite agony behind them. The woman could make him suffer all night if she wanted and the thought of wielding that kind of power over someone nearly put her over the edge. Nancy reached for the table just beside the man and heard his breathing quicken slightly and leaned down to whisper in his ear.

"Now."

His breathing quickened as vacant eyes stared into unseen faces that held his heart long ago. She sensed he was just about ready.

"Gwaed yn gosod i chi am ddim!" She drew a wicked-looking, black handled knife with a curved silver blade across the dying man's throat.

Nancy rose just in time for the warm, thick liquid to hit her chest and run down over her exposed breasts.

"Good," she moaned. "So good... ungh..."

She reached a climax that nearly buckled her knees and left her quivering in a half crouch, trying desperately not to fall over.

Nancy Seasons remained in that position until there was nothing left of him and then rose to her feet. She ran a finger across her breasts and licked off the liquid that ran down toward her navel. For a moment she stood in silence above his naked body and waited for his eyes to open and his jaw to slacken and fall agape.

"That was *wonderful,*" she said.

CHAPTER 5

D avis Mareth fell back into his seat on the westbound train and let out an exhausted sigh. He wished sleep would come, even if only for a few minutes, and take his mind far, far away from thoughts of Winterbourne and Nancy Seasons. Turning to the window, he closed his eyes and thought of the homeless man who shouted at him. What did he say?

Meth? There is just no pleasing some people.

He opened his eyes long enough to see a pretty, 20-something woman sit down in the seat next to him. Their eyes met and she smiled.

"Hey you're wearing scrubs too, what are the chances?"

"Oh, yeah," Davis replied, not quite knowing what to do with idle chatter. He didn't mind silences, uncomfortable or otherwise but he didn't want to talk; he wanted to sleep on the 45-minute trip home.

He noticed she wasn't really talking to him, as much as just talking, so he feigned sleeping, certain the real thing was just around the corner. Davis jerked awake after a few minutes, feeling uneasy just after the train went through the Rogers Street tunnel. He had slept for nearly 20 minutes and couldn't yet put a finger on it, but something was wrong. Wrong enough to wake him out of a near-death sleep.

"Wait, what?" Davis sounded mildly panicked. "What did you say?"

"I said I'm a nurse over at County. Why are you wearing scrubs?"

"Oh." Davis breathed a sigh. "I work over at Winterbourne. Just started."

"Oh," she said. "That's lovely. I hope to get into geriatrics. I just adore the elderly. If I had to say I had a calling that would be it. Old people are just so cute."

Davis looked at the back of the young nurse sitting beside him. Her brown hair was pinned up and the sun coming through the train car window highlighted the slenderness of her neck and made him wish he was more awake and interested in talking to her.

"Sorry," Davis began. "I'm just so tired and—"

"Nawr!" She turned and growled at him.

She leaned into him, examined him. Her eyes were like a porcelain doll's. The alabaster skin replaced with grey-green scales and bits of stray coarse black hair. She was more a *thing* than the pretty young woman when she sat down.

"Yr wyf yn eich helpu!" it shouted.

The young nurse creature's bitten off stub of a nose was inches away from his. Davis got the sense that, given the opportunity, she may gnaw a piece of flesh away from his face with the wicked teeth poorly contained within her thin angry lips.

Fear is an odd thing, it can make heroes out of the meek, and slobbering piles of goo out of the strongest of us. Terror, on the other hand, elicits only one response—leg it right now and get as far away from the source as humanly possible.

Davis decided in the five minutes that elapsed since this god-awful thing began to speak that he was not going to sit and listen any longer.

I am getting the holy blue fuck out of here. He tried to get up from his seat, but nothing happened. Undeterred, he made a conscious effort to get up and couldn't. No matter how hard he thought about it, he could not get up.

Okay, I'm tired. I'm so tired I'm not thinking straight. I'm going to get up out of this chair and I am going to move to a different car away from this horrible goddamned thing.

Davis' arm shot out to the right and came to rest firmly on his lap.

"Beth ydych chi'n ei fwyta nawr," the nurse thing said through snarling fangs.

Davis tried to sit up, more resolved than ever to get up and get off the train at the next stop.

"Beth ydych chi'n chwilio am absenoldeb?" it asked him and poked his chest with its green scaly talon.

Other things, twisted and ruined, obscene, gangling things with faces like smeared red paint on a chalk white canvas came by and spoke to him.

"Beth am ymlacio i chi ei wneud?"

Davis pushed back hard against his seat in an effort to get up and managed to shift about an inch. More obscenities came toward him from all directions, motioning to him and speaking over his protests. He twisted his head side to side, tried to get away from the hideous forms but wherever he looked, one was there to meet his gaze. Closing his eyes and trying to shut them out, only to have them pry his lids open with bony green fingers.

"Dim ond aros yn dawel."

I have got to get off this fucking train. Davis began to panic as the foul grotesques started to crowd around him.

"Please, I just want to get up." He cried now, anger and woe welled up and stung his eyes.

"I just want to go home. I just want to go home!"

He could feel his chest crushed under the weight of hopelessness that rose up in him like acidic vomit in the back of his throat, slowly eating away at his resolve.

"Os oedd gennych iddo beidio â brifo yr?" the abominations screamed and shook their claws at him.

"I am getting up off of this fucking train," he whispered, but for all of his fear and complaining, Davis Mareth did not budge. He thought of moving his arms, striking out at one of these creatures and making his way to the back of the train or pulling the emergency stop cord, something—anything to stop this. His arms were not interested in anything his brain had to say about movement and his legs became equally ignorant.

One of the people-shaped monstrosities came by and stood over Davis for a long time, tilting its head from side to side, looked him up and down. It gingerly grasped his hand in its claw and squatted down to meet him face to face.

"Rydych chi i gyd ar hyn o bryd," it said.

Davis felt an unexpected feeling of serenity come over him and although he desperately wanted to get up out of his chair, he thought it might be all right if he didn't do it right this second.

"Mae yna. Rydych chi i gyd ar hyn o bryd!"

Davis turned his face to the window and watched the tiny lights of the tunnel streak by. He looked back to the thing holding his hand and smiled. It bared fangs and hissed at him. Davis closed his eyes and knew in his bones he would never get off this train again.

CHAPTER 6

Davis felt a hand push his shoulder and immediately jerked upright, still not quite awake. He fully expected to see one of the heinous mutations but instead he looked at Nancy Seasons, which was just as frightening, maybe more.

"Mr. Mareth," she began. "I know that it can be difficult adjusting to the night shift so I will let you off this time, yes?"

"Yes, Ms. Seasons," Davis dutifully replied.

"But in future, I would recommend doing your sleeping at home and not at Winterbourne. Or I would recommend looking for another place to work, yes?"

"Yes, Ma'am."

He felt like a schoolboy being scolded for pulling pigtails at recess and was honestly surprised that he didn't tell Nancy Seasons where she could get off, but something was telling him he needed this job.

"Ms. Seasons?" Davis asked as she turned to leave.

"Yes Mr. Mareth?" Nancy replied.

"Will Jenn be here again this evening or am I working on my own?"

"You must have had some dream, Mr. Mareth," Nancy began. "This is your first nightshift and there is no one named Jenn working here as far as I know. You will be on your own tonight, as you will be on every other nightshift you work while you are here. I trust this is okay, yes?"

An awkward silence fell over them as tried to make sense of what he just heard. He looked at his watch, it read 1:35. Davis began his shift by doing paperwork and must have dozed off. Now he began to puzzle over the events that led him here. Staying awake for days on end came easily to him but never once experienced anything like this. What was it about this place that was different, what had caused him to dream something so vivid? And more to the point, what was Nancy Seasons still doing here at 1:30 in the morning? They had both been here early, but Davis at least tried to nap. There was dedication to the job but Davis was pretty certain Nancy didn't give a damn about anyone in this place, and if she was here this late it wasn't about eldercare.

He could forgo an argument about his experiences on the train. As real as it all seemed nothing that bizarre could have been real. But Jenn? How could he have dreamed something that vivid? He could still smell her cheap, Sears perfume and feel the warmth of her skin brushing up against his as they changed the residents that night.

"Of course," said Davis.

"Very good," Nancy's voice indicated it was not in the slightest way good. She produced a small, black and white composition book from her briefcase.

"Here is a list of the residents you will be caring for tonight and the times all of your activities need to be completed by, yes?"

"Thank you," Davis fumbled. "I'm sure this will come in very handy over the next few days."

She held the book just out of his reach and smirked as he left his arm hanging, not sure whether to put it back or not.

"Your security is inside this book, Mr. Mareth. Follow its instructions to the letter and you will have a future at Winterbourne. Deviate from it at all and I shudder to think of the consequences. Enjoy your shift, yes?"

Davis watched Nancy as she passed through the door way of the nurse's station. He was relieved that, if nothing else, he probably wouldn't need to speak to the frightening woman anymore tonight.

Nancy Seasons walked away from the nurse's station and headed back to her temporary office. She closed the door and stood in silence, looking out on to the courtyard through the room's small, lone window and took a deep breath. The air left her slowly as she sat down and opened the bottommost drawer of the massive desk. The drawer looked empty to the untrained eye, but Nancy Seasons knew better. She took a letter opener from the desktop and wedged it between the back wall and the bottom of the drawer, removing the plywood panel and revealing a large scrapbook with the word *Winterbourne* embossed across it in lettering that once had been gold and finely detailed, but now was peeled and partly missing. Nancy flipped calmly through a few pages until she found what she wanted. She looked intently at the article dated September 12, 1904.

Nurse Dies at Asylum

A nurse died yesterday of an apparent suicide at Winterbourne Home. No note was found with the body, but it is believed she had become involved in an inappropriate dalliance with a married staff doctor. Nurse Jennifer Henderson, 22 had no immediate family in the area. Funeral services are to be held at Winterbourne Home, burial to follow.

There was a picture with the article of a full-figured woman with dark hair wearing a nurse's uniform. Nancy flipped forward a few more pages and found another article that grabbed her attention.

Death at Winterbourne

Winterbourne home was the scene of a desperate double tragedy yesterday as a young doctor apparently went mad and strangled an inmate to death and then took his own life in his office. Dr. Charles A. Douglas had recently been employed as head psychiatrist at

Winterbourne for only a short time and was reportedly struggling to cope with the rigors of his new role.

There will be a brief memorial service held in the grand hall of Winterbourne on Saturday the 21st.

Nancy Seasons looked at the picture that accompanied the article, she recognized the doctor's face from photographs around the building, but the nurse in the picture grabbed her attention and held it. It was the same nurse from the previous scrap book article. She was certain of it, though written in pen across the bottom of the article was "March 1918—lacked the strength to finish."

She flipped through the rest of the scrapbook looking at various articles about the sordid history of Winterbourne Home; its walls stained with the blood and suffering of the helpless. From its opening year to the day it shut its doors shut, the place was marred by accidents, murder and general carnage and someone had taken a keen interest in documenting all of it in this scrapbook, complete with handwritten notes.

Nancy had been transfixed by the book from the day she'd first seen the old director looking through it. He had told her about the desk and all of its secrets, including the scrapbook, explaining one day it would be hers so she better learn all she could from it. She pored over it almost daily and was immediately struck by the appearance of the dark-haired nurse in all of the articles in the scrapbook. From beginning to end, there were drawings and photographs of the same woman. At first, Nancy thought it must be women from the same family; a mother and daughters perhaps, or even sisters, but it wasn't a family, it was the same robust, dark-haired woman in all of these articles.

However she wasn't shocked by this discovery. Nancy Seasons was taken under the wing of the previous director—a man who was so singularly skilled at portraying himself as a kindly, compassionate man who loved his charges better than himself that nobody had the slightest idea what a loathsome, malevolent reptile he really was. He had introduced her to such pleasures and depravities that nothing shocked her anymore. No, Nancy was intrigued. How could this chubby woman escape that which was inescapable? What knowledge did she possess that Nancy did not?

Nancy set the scrapbook back inside the drawer and replaced its false bottom. She closed her eyes, leaned back on her chair and thought of the woman in the pictures. The dark haired woman wasn't a ghost, Nancy was at least fairly certain of that, but she clearly had talents far beyond those currently held by Ms. Nancy Seasons and that chapped her ass in the worst way. Nancy was also fairly certain that this portly, non-ghost woman thing poked her nose around Winterbourne's newest employee and the window was quickly closing on the director's chance to use Davis Mareth for all he was worth. And she would be damned if she would miss her one chance for real power because of the meddling of some long-forgotten fat girl.

CHAPTER 7

D avis pushed the towel cart down the dark hallway, thumbing his way through the book Nancy gave him. He stopped in the middle of the hall. "No way," he said. "There is no goddamned way I can believe that. I can't believe any of that. I dreamed a whole day? Are you nuts?"

He halfway expected to hear a voice telling him he wasn't crazy and it was real, but when no voice answered he felt a little defeated and thought just maybe it was all in his mind. Davis looked at the book and felt a cold sweat creep across the back of his neck when he saw the first entry; *Mrs. L. Helm rm 107.*

"Goddammit!" he said, and threw the book to the floor.

Davis had only experienced true fear a few times in his life. Not that fear you feel when somebody jumps out and yells "BOO," only to take off the werewolf mask. Or when your girlfriend tells you she's pregnant and lets you stew for an hour or so before saying she was interested to see how you'd react. But the type of bona fide fear you feel laying alone in bed and hearing the handle of a locked door angrily rattled from outside. The type of fear that requires superhuman concentration to function beyond. In that the second or two that your brain shuts off and panic moves in, between when the rope reaches its apex, when you wonder how long it will take to die after your face meets the rocks below and when the line springs back up toward the bridge from which you just bungee jumped.

He began to feel electric shocks of panic grip him as unfamiliar noises filled his ears from every direction he turned and suddenly he became very aware there were things all around him, unfriendly things he reasoned, frightful shadows moving and beginning to take shape only to disappear when he tried to focus on them. Trying to quell the howling fear inside, he took a deep breath and picked up Nancy's black and white book. He could feel his heart thundering in his chest and thought he would blackout if he couldn't tame the pale dread spreading like a hoarfrost in his brain and start doing anything other than think about how terrifying all of this was.

Davis closed his eyes and cautiously moved to Room 107 where he could hear voices from behind the door, voices he wasn't quite certain weren't all in his head. *What the hell is going on in there?* Summoning up enough tenacity to step toward the door, he reached out for it in the darkness.

He gripped the doorknob and felt the fear rip up his spine and play hell on his imagination as the handle was yanked from his grip.

"Gotcha, shit eyes!" the old woman in the hospital gown yelled.

"Wait!" Davis hollered.

He was a little surprised at himself when he realized he was raising his hands to strike out at the voice and jerked them back only after noticing it was a tiny, geriatric, nearly naked woman behind the door.

"Oh hey," the old woman said. "Hey, are you all right, dear? You look as if you've just seen a ghost."

"I think I might have," said Davis. "I'm here to change you."

"Change me into what?" she asked.

"Change your... you know, your brief," Davis said sheepishly. He pointed in the general direction of her crotch.

"Ah, you mean you're here to change my diaper," she said.

Davis noticed that she put the emphasis on the first half of the word every time she said it.

"I'm not supposed to call them that, it's undignified," Davis explained.

"Wearing the goddamned things is even more undignified. Anyway, I don't."

"You don't—" Davis started to ask.

"I don't wear a diaper. I haven't pissed in my pants since I was two."

Davis stood and looked at her thinking she seemed awfully lucid for someone this place. He came here with notions they were all deep in the throes of dementia or some other mania, wandering around talking to walls and picking imaginary change off the carpeted floor. This woman wasn't anything like that. She seemed aware of what was going on around her and fully capable of deciding what her part in all of it was going to be.

"You're in my book," Davis said to her.

"What book?" the old woman asked.

Davis held up the book for her to see and explained what Nancy Seasons told him.

"You'd do very well to just follow this book and do as your told, yes?" the old woman said in a perfect impression of Nancy Seasons.

Davis laughed and felt the weight of fear lift. He felt he might actually cry from the lightness he felt in the void it left.

"L. Helm," the old woman growled and turned away from the book. "Cripes, I don't even get a first name?"

"They're all just first initials," Davis agreed. "I guess she thought I didn't need to know anybody's name."

"Don't kid yourself," said the old woman. "Miss Nancy Seasons, if you please, doesn't give a hoot in hell about anybody in this place except Nancy Seasons. She gave you this book for a reason and it wasn't to help you out. Something stinks here."

"I thought you didn't wear a diaper?" Davis asked in mocking seriousness.

"Shut up," she said playfully and smacked his arm. It felt more like a pat on the back from her and he needed one.

Davis liked the old woman. She reminded him of a black-and-white movie, where all the men were a little out of place and all the women talked tough and didn't take shit from anybody. He knew if he didn't get moving soon, he would be eating a boatload of shit, served up by Ms. Nancy Seasons, yes?

"Mrs. Helm," he began. "I really need to get moving. I have a lot of work to do before the morning. I'm sure there are people that do need to be changed."

"Lois," she said.

"I'm sorry?" Davis asked.

"Mrs. Helm was my mother, my name is Lois."

"Oh," said Davis a little shocked.

"Some of us have stopped making sense, honey, but we haven't stopped being people."

"Right, sorry Lois."

Davis turned to leave her room when he thought to ask her the question that gnawed at him since before he entered.

"Lois, who were you talking to before I came in?"

"Well, I was talking to you I guess, but I thought you were him," Lois said.

"You though I was who?" Davis asked.

"I thought you were the man who lives in my closet," Lois replied as though it were common knowledge that there was a man living in her closet.

"We dated a long time ago but we don't talk much anymore. He's kind of an asshole now and I didn't want him coming in here this way."

He had to look. As a rule, Davis knew men didn't go around living in old women's closets but this was not a place where people were accustomed to living by reasonable sets of rules any longer. Anything could be possible in a place like this. He opened the closet door and was very relieved to find a few tattered outfits, a stained nightgown and a ratty pair of shoes. There was no evidence of this closet being a dwelling for anyone ever. It didn't look as though it had spent any time being anything other than a closet. Davis smiled and told Lois he would check in on her later.

Okay, he thought. Maybe a smidge of crazy.

Davis headed out the door and consulted the black and white composition book; Mrs. K. Nesbitt, rm 110. E.O.L. was the next entry after Lois. He had no idea what E.O.L. meant but was confident he would figure it out once she was in her room.

The young man wasn't certain how she had done it but Lois Helm had made notations of her own in the margins of the book. Beside Mrs. K Nesbitt's name she had written, *This old bird is on the way out. Make sure she smells good.*

Nervously he tried to turn the handle to the door as quietly as he could, feeling more than a little foolish. A grenade could go off just beside the nightstand and most of the people in Winterbourne would never hear it. He crept into the room expecting to see a motionless elderly body lying on a bed. Instead he froze, paralyzed by what he saw. Davis wanted to move away from it, wanted to turn and flee but his legs would not move him. He wanted to look away from the sight of it but was drawn closer, as if he drove slowly past some ghastly car wreck.

Mrs. K. Nesbitt of room 110 laid motionless in bed, she was not alone. Sitting on top of her, straddling her chest, was one of the apparitions Davis saw on the train, and now he could see it for all it was.

Smaller than an adult, he thought. Maybe the size of an eight or nine-year-old child. It was greyish-green and scaly, like a lizard, but with wisps of coarse hair covering its body from shoulders to short, squat legs. Davis thought it was more like an ape than any kind of reptile he had ever seen. The arms were too long for its body and though they looked sinewy and powerful, they gave it a gangly appearance emphasized by the long slender fingers on each hand. It was only the monstrous claws that capped all 10 fingers that stopped the thing from looking completely farcical. It had black, lifeless eyes too large for its face and reminded Davis alien images that seemed to be keenly interested in the rectal cavities of hillbillies across America. An impression reinforced by the thing's oversized, bulbous head. It had hair, if you could call it hair, long and it ended in points that reminded Davis of dreadlocks—if they were worn by a porcupine. The terrible thing noticed Davis and smiled at him, revealing a slathering mouth and needle-pointed teeth.

"I'm sorry." Davis did not know what else to say and hurriedly turned to leave the room.

"Peidiwch â gadael," it hissed. "Aros a gweld!"

Davis stood in the room, horrified and transfixed by the spectacle happening a foot away from him. The grey-green obscenity sat atop Mrs. Nesbitt, breathed deeply then pressed its mouth against hers. It took hold of her blue flannel gown and shook until Davis thought she might snap at the waist. The needle toothed anomaly drew the old woman's face close again and latched its mouth onto her. Davis could see the blood begin to run down her chin and without warning, the loathsome thing drove its claws straight into the old woman's chest ripping and tearing away bits of her with hideous abandon. Blood splattered the walls and chunks of the old woman's flesh slid down in a gruesome tableau. Davis felt a flash of anger and a small spark of bravery grew into a flame of wrath as he stepped forward to save Mrs. Kubrick any further indignities, only to be thrown roughly against the woman's closet by unseen hands. The thing climbed off Mrs. Nesbitt and Davis could see, for the first time, that despite squat legs and thin, sinewy arms, it would have been more than a formidable opponent had it chosen to meet his advance head on.

The awful thing glanced at him as it, opened the door to the old woman's closet and stepped inside. The door closed and all was silent. Davis looked to the figure on the bed. *My God, the blood. There is so much blood.* He ran out of the room and mindlessly around the halls, looking for a linen closet. After finding one, he gathered up a handful of sheets and towels and hurried back to Mrs. K. Nesbitt's room.

He opened the door and felt his knees wobble below him. "What the fuck?"

There was no blood, there was no gore dripping off the walls. Just the late Mrs. K. Nesbitt of room 110 Winterbourne Home and she laid peacefully on her bed looking, for all intents and purposes, as though asleep. If Davis hadn't known better, he'd have sworn she died in her sleep. He nervously walked over to the bed and saw she was indeed dead and not torn apart. In fact, Davis thought, there was a faint smile on her face.

Davis was prepared for this eventuality—someone dying while he worked—but he didn't think it would happen on his first night. He soaked a towel in warm water from the bathroom faucet and began to wash her. It didn't disturb him, handling the old dead woman, though maybe it should. He finished washing and started to wrap her in a sheet and thought about what he'd seen an hour prior. A shudder ran up his spine when he remembered how the thing sat on top of her chest and spoke to him just before it tore her to pieces. Nearly done, he wrapped her head and went to call the duty nurse. Mr. K. Nesbitt of room 110 was no longer, but to look at the half-opened, droopy eyes, you might think she drifted off to sleep. It was the dullness inside those eyes that betrayed any notion she was still an ongoing concern. The light had left her eyes. Davis closed the lids only to have them open. He tried a second time with the same result and let out a little snicker. If Mrs. K. Nesbitt wanted to go into the next life with her eyes half-opened, which she clearly did, who was Davis to stop her?

The weary care worker walked toward the Nurse's station feeling numb. Not because of the death of the old woman, it was a nursing home after all. He thought a nursing home was kind of a geriatric roach motel. Granny checks in but she never checks out. No, it wasn't the old woman's death that twisted in his guts, nor even the vicious scaly freak thing brutalizing her only to be gone as quickly as it had come—though that was right up there with things he didn't ever need to experience again.

It was Jenn and his shift with her that left him baffled. He was exhausted enough to dream up the monster that eats old ladies, but to hallucinate and interact with that hallucination over a whole day? That wasn't sleep deprivation—that was out to lunch. There was something going on here and, real or not, it was tied to her.

"Mrs. Nesbitt is gone," Davis told the nurse in a somber tone.

"Were you there when it happened, or did you find her?" the nurse asked him.

Davis swallowed. "I was there when she passed."

"Was it a good death?"

He stood in stunned silence, looking at her puzzled expression.

"It isn't a difficult question," she said flatly. "You were there in the room with her when she passed. If she suffered it was not a good death. Was it a good death? I have to chart it."

Davis felt the words leave his lips before realizing he was saying them.

"Yes," he began. "It was a good death. If your idea of a good death is some kind of goggle-eyed, Rastafarian, lizard-ape fucking thing ripping her to pieces is good, then it was an absolute peach of a goddamned death!"

"Davis?" the nurse shouted.

"Wait, what? Oh, sorry," Davis sputtered, waken from his daydream. "She went quietly."

It was true; the old woman didn't make a peep. Between the flesh ripping and the rapacious, marrow-sucking, evil of it all, it was the grey-green thing that made all of the noise.

"You should try to get some sleep after your shift," she said. "You look like shit."

He went through the last 45 minutes of his shift without incident. Nobody died and nobody told him anymore about the inhabitants of their closets. In fact, nobody stirred at all, but the uneasiness he had been feeling dug its claws firmly into his neck and refused to leave him. As he changed clothes, his thoughts were of the handsome woman with dark hair who he apparently imagined. Davis Mareth walked out of the building and down the steps he could feel eyes staring at him, staring through him. He whipped around to look back at the windows, expecting to see her, but it wasn't Jenn.

Nancy Seasons stood at the window of her office, her mouth moving around silent words, her face trained directly on him. Her eyes were rolled so far back in her head that only the whites were visible but still her head followed his every movement. She raised her hand, pointed two pudgy fingers at him and zeroed in on him with her cadaverous, pallid eyes. The extended fingers moved up to her face and she drew them from the left side of her temple, across her eyes and stopping at the right temple, her milky gaze never moving from his face. She moved back from the window slowly and smoothly, and disappeared into the blackness of the room.

Davis hurried down the stairs of Winterbourne and out into the street. He looked up the street at the people waiting at the bus stop.

"Taxi!" he waved at a passing cab.

The cab stopped and he clambered into the backseat.

"19 Pitt Bridge Way," he told the driver and fell back into the seat.

CHAPTER 8

Nancy Seasons awoke on the floor of her small office and tried to collect herself. She looked at her watch - 7:25 AM. She hadn't slept for nearly two days but time was running out. Nancy wondered why there always seemed to be time for the things that needed her attention, but the things she really wanted to do—the things that would change her life—were always being short-changed. The director went back to her desk and picked up the phone. As she dialled the extension, she drummed her fingers impatiently against her desk.

"Room 125 down. I'll be there in 10 minutes."

"Yes, Ms. Seasons," said a male voice.

Nancy hung up and walked out toward the double doors that led to a section still under construction. There were two more soon-to-be identical wards down this unfinished hallway, as well as a full-sized office for her. At the far end of the hallway stood the service elevator and, after pushing the call button and several tedious moments of waiting, she stepped inside. She pushed the down-arrow and hummed a melancholy tune she couldn't entirely remember, until the doors opened. After looking to either side of the door, knowing full well there was never anyone down there but her, she stepped out. The housekeeping staff refused to come down unless a dozen more lights were put up and it was exorcised of all the ghoulish, stained mental hospital equipment. Nancy refused to do those things. She saw the basement of Winterbourne and decided it would be perfect for her newfound pursuits, she feigned concern for the well-being of the staff and had the laundry moved to the first floor.

The director walked through the double doors directly in front of her, entered the small bathroom to her right and stripped off her clothes. She turned on the cold water and pulled her favourite thick, pink comb from her purse. After dousing her head with cold water, she combed her hair straight back and took out the clear crystal jar containing the viscous black liquid. Nancy took a generous amount and with two fingers, smeared the black goop from one temple to another, blacking out her eyes. She then took another handful and smeared a pattern in the middle of her chest extending outward to both her breasts. Nancy opened the doors on the bottom of the vanity and took out a large, black leather bag. Her heart delighted when she opened the bag and saw the wickedness within it. She carefully selected a knife with an eight-inch curved blade, stepped out of the bathroom, then walked toward the figure sitting beyond the archway in front of her.

The old woman sat silently in the chair, helpless and afraid and craning her head to better hear the approaching footsteps. Unseeing eyes and useless legs had betrayed her long ago and left her a victim of trust—tonight would make her no less a casualty.

Nancy Seasons walked up to the old woman and gently kissed her forehead.

"Who's there?" the old woman asked.

Nancy remained silent as she walked behind the woman.

"Are you a relative?" The old woman called out, moving her head from side to side, trying to get a bearing on where the person was in the room.

Nancy moved closer and pressed her breasts against the back of the woman's head. She felt herself become aroused and let out a small, trembling gasp.

"I can feel you there. Please tell me who you are."

Nancy stopped in her tracks and tried to remain silent, quivering with the anticipation of what was about to happen. She walked forward and smelled the old woman's hair. She smelled fear. It was delicious and made her knees weak.

"Please," the old woman wept. "I'm frightened and I just want to go back to my room."

"Shh." Nancy breathed.

"I can hear you," said the old woman with a sudden air of insurgency. "Take me back to my room."

Nancy knew this was it; she could smell the sweet panic dripping with false bravado. She leaned in and licked the ancient lips and felt herself reach a frenzied peak.

"Gwaed yn gosod i chi am ddim," Nancy said then drove the knife home, deep into the old woman's throat. She held it firm as the old woman's life drained from her in a grievous death spasm then knelt down in front of her to catch the final splatters as they pulsed from the moribund senior.

Nancy walked back through the double doors and down the hallway to the old laundry room where she took a hose from a hook on the wall and attached it to one of the rinse sinks. She began to wash off the black viscous goo and the old woman's blood. Confusion dogged her and that pissed her off and the coldness of the water served to fuel the heat of her anger even more. *How many more of these old cranks before it is enough? Have I not done everything as he had told me or am I just wandering in the dark, decreasing the aging population?* She picked up the phone from the wall and dialled.

"There is a mess down here that needs tending to, yes?" she said and hung up.

Dressing quickly, she headed back to her office and took a seat behind the big oak desk. She opened the trick drawer again and took out the scrapbook. Nancy was certain she had followed his instructions, certain that she was doing as he had told her all those years ago, yet here she was, not any different nor any more forceful than she ever had been. Not that she minded doing away with the old buggers. That was a pleasant little bonus as far as she was concerned, but if it wasn't going to get her any closer to the real power she deserved, then it was no different than screwing the young council members. It was fun but in the end, it was like eating a gourmet meal on an unwashed plate. Gratifying while it lasted but once it was over, what remained was grubby and repellent.

She thumbed through the pages of the scrapbook until she found a letter written by her predecessor. The man who'd taught her everything, but lacked the courage to act on that knowledge. *A tragic weakness,* Nancy thought. She would never be that weak, not now after having gone so far.

She read the letter;

My dear Nancy,

I have learned a secret, the method by which a person could wield a power so unimaginable, I shudder to think what I would become if I possessed it. Imagine, the power of Thanatos himself! Think of it, Nancy! The power to control death, to lock away the Servant of the Void and assume the full mantle of his power.

The eldritch tome was given to me by my predecessor and he in turn was given it by his, but it was written in an ancient tongue that took me years to understand. I have transcribed it into plain language for you where I could, and made certain all the instructions are plain, down to the symbols and specific phrases, how to pronounce them and when to say them. The rest is fairly straightforward, but here's the rub…

The text clearly says that at least 12 souls are needed to start to shift the balance between the living and the dead. Twelve unclaimed, innocent souls and Death will take notice and come to claim what is rightfully his.

This is the tricky bit, as long as there is no successor to take Death's place, no Mortal Scion. He is trapped and must submit to your will for as long as you possess the book. If you could find out who Death's heir is and make him one of the 12, you couldn't possibly fail.

Nancy, I was unable to complete this ritual in my entire tenure here, nor were any of my colleagues successful. None of us could ever find the successor to the Servant of the Abyss, he was hidden much too well. Nor did any of them, or myself, come close to the level of ruthlessness and malignant determination that you possess. If anyone can accomplish this it is you, dear, dear Nancy.

When you are ready, I have written the translation in the back of a simple black and white composition book, which I have put in my desk. You have my absolute faith and if you succeed, I will see you again I'm sure.

Yours,
D.

The first time she met the director Nancy walked into his office and applied for a job cleaning rooms. The attraction was evident even then and the young woman knew in a heartbeat that, it was only a matter of time before she could get him to do anything for her. She went back to his office at night and had sex with him on top of the big oak desk. Within a month she was his private secretary, and within a year the assistant director. He admired her drive and wanton lust for power, almost as much as the blouses that barely contained her chest.

He began to tell her the stories that haunted Winterbourne Home and how those who came before him were all guilty of unspeakable, unnatural things that resulted in the deaths of several residents and staff members. When she didn't seem upset or disgusted by the stories and rumours he shared but seemed intrigued, he decided to tell her about the book.

Nancy Seasons looked back to the letter in a panic.

"…*a simple black and white composition book…*"

"Oh shit!" Nancy spat.

CHAPTER 9

D avis Mareth collapsed into his apartment and threw his backpack on the couch. The black and white composition book fell out and Davis feared Nancy Seasons would flay him alive if he didn't possess the damn thing every waking moment he was on the ward. Carefully picking it up, he began to open the front cover but thought better of it, or maybe he was just too tired to think about anything but crawling into bed and letting sleep take him. Davis gave the book no more thought and returned it to the backpack, zipping the top securely. He thought about just how tired he was. It had only been eight hours but the sense that he hadn't a clue what he was doing, coupled with Mrs. Nesbitt's death left him feeling like he had worked a triple shift.

Something he read a lifetime ago suddenly came to him, something about someone collapsing onto a bed out of sheer exhaustion and wondered if he had reached that point yet. He supposed, after a bit of shin brushed the edge of the mattress and the rest of his body crumpled on the bed like a paper lunch bag, that point had been reached. Davis slept, but it was far from restful. There was an awful sense of disconnection that made it feel like the body was asleep long before the head made contact with the pillow, but his mind was already well on its way back to Winterbourne and beyond. He was standing at the foot of the stairs of the center tower, it was near dawn and the smell of mist hung heavy in the cool air.

Davis walked up the stairs and stood in front of two large, ornate doors of oak and stained glass. On the left door was the image of a small, beautiful boy. Large, dark feathered wings extended from his back and a small sword hung from his waist. The right door portrayed the image of an identically beautiful, dark-winged girl pouring a black liquid out of an ornate silver amphora. Davis reached to open the left-hand door, only to have it swing open before he could reach the handle.

He was standing in a large, white room filled with row upon row of hard high back chairs. Some of them were occupied by people of varying ages. Some reading, some looking at watches, and some sighing heavily trying not to sleep. It reminded Davis of a gigantic waiting room. Along the northwest wall was a massive L-shaped desk that seemed excessively tall. So tall, in fact, that you'd have to back away several steps from the desk to speak to anyone sitting at it. It seemed to Davis like a parody of a courtroom, where this gigantic desk's occupant would look down on the poor bugger unlucky enough to stand before it.

There were lines laid out two feet in front of the desk, extending its whole length in either direction. Davis could see the outlines of people working away at these desks but couldn't tell if they were men or women. As he approached, his heart raced. There were hundreds of them, the things he saw on the train and ripped apart the old woman. They were wandering around the big, white room carrying envelopes and other bits of paper going about the business of whatever it was that psychotic, spiny, reptilian apes do when they get to the office. He noticed a ticket machine in the center of the chair-filled area with a large sign above it reading "Take a Number Please." Davis took a ticket without looking at it and sat. The chairs were uncomfortable, hard-backed, modular plastic that had a tendency to push you forward. If you began to relax, even slightly, you were likely to wind up face first on the floor.

A bell rang and a voice came over a loud speaker.

"Now serving number... four," the voice said politely.

Davis looked around the seating area and thought there were fewer people here now than when he came in a moment ago. There couldn't be more than five or ten of them and he was certain he wouldn't be waiting here long. He reached into his pocket and took out his ticket, number 537; well at least he was already asleep.

One of the spindly nightmare creatures stared at him as it hurried by with a bundle of papers and went excitedly to another creature sitting behind the big desk. Davis couldn't hear what they were saying, but the conversation seemed excited. Soon two more joined them and now they was a quartet of pointing, arguing, and jostling, Rastafarian, lizard-chimpanzee things. One of them came out from behind the desk and ambled over to him.

"Mr. Mareth?" it asked.

"Yes?" Davis replied.

The thing's manner of speech was decidedly middle-class English, and Davis thought if he closed his eyes and opened them again he would be looking at a man with a small moustache in a gray flannel suit wearing a bowler hat.

"Mr. Mareth, you needn't wait out here, he's been expecting you, Go right in."

A chorus of sighs went up from the seating room as Davis stood up and followed the thing behind the desk.

Davis tried not to look at the people waiting and throwing irritated, dirty looks his way. He was honestly surprised that, for all the anger in their looks, not a single comment was made. They remained strangely silent.

"Asshole," a seated man called after him.

Nearly silent, Davis thought.

He stepped through hospital-style double crash doors into an impossibly long, poorly lit hallway that looked like it wound through a castle instead of office building. The walls looked like they were made of limestone and were covered in dust and dirt, and in the low light, they looked faintly green.

Davis couldn't reason why, but from the start of it all he had been aware it was a dream. At least on the surface. He wasn't bothered by or afraid of anything he saw or experienced. It was liberating to walk with an attitude of invincibility.

"I just love the décor," he said to the emptiness.

"Thank you," the voice said. "This is your dream, you should love it."

Davis stopped walking and stood motionless, suddenly very afraid of where he was and what might happen if he continued to walk down the dingy hallway.

"Nothing is going to happen," the voice called out gently. "You are completely safe here. You have to trust that if I wished it, you would have been the late Davis Mareth the second you walked through the door."

"That's not very reassuring," Davis called out. "Why shouldn't I just turn around and haul ass out of here?"

"Because nobody ever gets hurt in their dreams."

There was a comfortable familiarity in the voice, he was certain he had heard it before, but couldn't remember just where.

"Besides," said the voice. "I am a really nice guy and if you leave now, you'll have missed your chance to meet me. Now can you, ah, just get down here please?"

Davis walked slowly down the hallway, not entirely trusting whoever was behind the voice. It seemed like he had been walking a very long time and he had the impression that he had walked downhill because now it felt like he walked uphill, and it was getting tougher.

"Just a little farther," the voice promised. "It will be worth it."

It was beginning to grate on him, not being able to remember just where he had heard this man's voice before. Davis closed his eyes and tried to roll them back far enough into his skull that he might see the answer. He couldn't and so he moved onward, muttering to himself.

Then he came, at last, to the end of the stonework hallway and looked up at a massive set of spiral stairs.

"Impressive," said Davis.

"Thank you," said the voice. "We just had them done."

Davis put his foot on the first step, they felt odd. Not like the granite they looked to be made of, but softer, almost squishy. He grabbed the handrail and went up cautiously, feeling his feet might come out from under him at any time. For all the length of the hallway. The stairs were short by comparison. He was at the top in no time.

The top of the stairs opened into a large corner room with two bay windows on each of the opposing walls. In the middle of the room sat a huge oak desk, remarkably like the desk Nancy Seasons had in her office. Davis was pretty certain that, since this was a dream, this was in fact the desk from Nancy Seasons' office. He could see a person sitting at the desk with his back to the stairs—or at least he could see that person's arms. The chair he sat in was a high-backed, black leather chair that looked like something a bank manager might sit in to exemplify how large and important he was, and how small and insignificant you were.

Davis already had the feeling he was not about to like the person sitting in that chair, whoever or whatever he was. He saw an arm come out from the front of the high-backed chair and reach for a coffee cup sitting on the desk. The arm was wearing the sleeve of a tan and brown patterned sweater rather than the suit jacket Davis thought he should be seeing.

He noticed that beside the cup lay a black and white composition book like the one currently sitting in the top of his backpack. The arm replaced the coffee cup and reached for the book. The chair began to turn toward him as Davis moved into the office. He could feel his chest tightening as more of the figure in the chair became visible. As the chair finished turning, Davis smiled and remembered where he had heard the voice before.

CHAPTER 10

"**D**on't you ever sleep at home?" the voice asked Davis.

"What?" Davis asked through barely opened eyes and peeled his face from the nurse's desk he had been sleeping on like gum stuck to the bottom of a shoe. He desperately tried to focus on the face behind the voice.

"I asked, don't you ever sleep at home?"

Jenn Henderson poked his ribs and Davis was suddenly very aware that he was not home in his bed.

"Hey," she said. "You still here?"

Davis flew off the chair, eyes wide with fear.

"Who are you and what the fuck is going on in this goddamned place?" he bawled.

He stood staring at Jenn, relieved, almost happy, to see the dark haired woman again, but at this moment his brain was flipping between the shock of seeing her and the general bewilderment of being ripped from such a vivid dream. Muddled, his emotions beat across him like waves of summer heat. He felt the blood leave his head.

"You can't tell me that carrot wasn't driving the Cadillac!" He stretched out his hand for support, grabbed handfuls of fresh air instead.

"Are you okay?" Jenn asked. "You don't look so hot."

"I look just like every other fjong in this bnorn."

He felt the floor rise up to meet him with an indignant smack on the cheek. His head bounced up and the floor smacked his cheek a second time. Davis stared at Jenn's shoes and thought they looked very clean for having been here as long as she had, just before all went black.

"Welcome back," said Jenn. "I thought you were a goner for a moment there."

Davis sat bolt upright and tried to get up off of the floor, but gravity and the feeling in the pit of his stomach won out and he fell back down.

"Take it easy," she said. "You're all right but you need to rest a bit."

"Who the hell are you?"

She stuck out her hand to shake his. "Jenn Henderson," she said. "Real live dead girl."

"How?" Davis asked.

His head really began to spin. On the one hand, the entire time with her was not a dream, so at least he wasn't losing his mind, but on the other, Davis was speaking to a dead woman that, almost certainly, he was developing a crush on.

"Tough to explain," she began. "Let's say that I died here a while back and can't seem to find the door to get out."

"Are you cursed?" Davis asked. "Did you do something terrible and now you must wander the earth for all of eternity as punishment?"

"You watch too many movies," she said. "The only terrible thing I ever did was screw a doctor who was the director. I made an offhand remark about strange things going on at this hospital and the next thing I know, I'm trussed up in a room in the basement and he shows up with an orderly who proceeds to choke the life out of me. The bastard had the orderly string me up after I was dead and announced that he found me dead. My poor mother thought my soul was going to be damned to hell. You know, in a way, she was right."

Davis listened to her in rapt silence, trying very hard not to look as though he snuck school boy glances at her chest, which he was.

"Stop looking at my chest fella, the bank's closed," she said in mock anger.

Davis' face flushed when she laughed at his embarrassment. There was no malice in it, Jenn's laughter was pure and innocent and it erupted from her like fresh summer rain.

"Wait, what?" asked Davis. "What do you mean he had an orderly strangle you?"

"He was the director of medicine, the youngest one ever at the time. He was powerful and he was cruel and he delighted in both. People feared him and his power to take away their jobs, the orderlies especially. He dangled their jobs and the promise of extra money in front of them so they didn't dare question anything he wanted from them. That allowed him to indulge in every sick fantasy he ever had without a single consequence."

"And you stuck around until you found justice? So your soul could go on in peace?"

"There is no justice in this place," Jenn said ominously. "Only death."

"That's a little creepy," Davis said.

"Did you just say my immortal soul's torment is a little creepy?" she asked, sounding slightly indignant.

No!" Davis feared he would upset her. "Okay, maybe a little."

She laughed at him. "I stay because I couldn't leave. I tried, in the beginning, then I just kind of gave in and got on with it."

"What happened to the director and the orderly?"

She looked at a point beyond Davis' head.

"The director became the chief administrator of the whole hospital, as everyone suspected he would and continued to use his power like a weapon. People were hired and fired without warning or simply disappeared from Winterbourne. And once everyone was sufficiently terrified of him, he continued exploring his darker passions unchecked. A lot of people died around this place to fuel his sick pastimes. He called them 'necessary experiments' but everybody knew what was happening in that room had nothing to do with medicine. The orderly never forgave himself for what he did, nor did he ever tell anyone about it. He became cold and distant to the people around him who couldn't understand the burdens he carried.

"His only child, the only reason he ever agreed to do as the director asked, disappeared rather suspiciously. Nobody ever came out and said it but the whole town, even his wife, suspected he had something to do with it. After that, he gave up on himself and waited for death to take him while he watched everyone around him go first. As far as I know, he is still alive, suffering and still waiting."

"He should suffer."

Davis tried to sound cavalier.

"Why?" asked Jenn. "Why should he suffer, because he killed me?"

"Umm... yeah," Davis muttered, not quite understanding where she was going.

"He killed me, yes," she began "But it was someone else guiding his hands. Should he suffer for all of eternity because he wanted things to be better for his family? His heart was in the right place even if his hands were not."

Davis stood there, stunned. He wanted to say something, anything to let her know he understood, but he didn't. He didn't understand any of it. If he had been murdered, by anyone and he was left to hang around he would make it his lifelong... okay, his after-lifelong obsession to get all the revenge he could.

"Don't kid yourself," Jenn said. "I wanted revenge and I almost burned myself out looking to get it."

"Wait, what? Are you reading my mind?"

"Kinda yes, kinda no," she said. "One of the perks of being me."

"I have so many things I want- I need to ask you," Davis said eagerly.

"I know," Jenn said to him motherly. "And I can answer some of them, but there are other things that I just don't have the answers to."

"Who does?" asked Davis.

"You'll find out soon."

"That's not fair."

"Sorry," Jenn said "I have my instructions."

"Instructions?"

"Later," she reassured him. "Look, one thing I have to tell you is watch out for Nancy Seasons. She is not what she seems. Well, okay she is exactly what she seems and very much worse. She's up to something. I just haven't figured out what yet. Just don't trust her, at all."

"I don't," Davis said. "I got a strange feeling from her the day I met her and it stuck with me. She makes my skin crawl."

She looked at her watch. "I've got to get going."

Davis thought it a little odd that a dead woman was concerned about promptness.

"Go where?" he asked her. "It's not like you have a busy day ahead of you, is it?"

"That's what you know. Do you think that once you're gone, you have nothing but time until the end of time?"

"Isn't that how it goes?" he asked.

"Far from it," she stated. "I have more to do now than I ever did when I was alive, and I was a nurse in a mental hospital."

"Are you still a nurse?" Davis asked.

"No," she said. "I would say I was more of a secretary now."

"Really?" Davis asked in an astonished tone. "For who?"

"Tough to explain," Jenn said flatly. "But you'll find out. I wish I could tell you more—I'm dying to but I just can't. Not right now anyway. See you soon."

She stood, headed for the door then stopped and turned.

"Look, it's going to be another tough night but you can get through it. Stay strong, they need you to be. We all do."

With that she opened the door and stepped outside.

"Through the door?" Davis sputtered.

"Through the door," She stated matter-of-factly. "Do I look like Casper to you?"

"You can't walk through walls, then?"

"Pfft," Jenn rebuked. "I wish. Do you know how much time that would save? See ya, kid."

The door closed behind her and Davis sat, feeling a little deflated. There was so much he wanted to tell Jenn and it wasn't shyness that stood in the way but interrupting meant she would have to stop talking and he really liked listening to the sound of the woman's voice.

It's going to be another tough night. How much tougher could it get than hallucinating monkey lizards that butcher grannies, and travelling from home to work in your sleep?

He left the office, headed out onto the floor and all seemed quiet and peaceful. Davis thought of Lois, the woman he had met on his first night and decided to see if she was still awake.

"Jimmy!" Lois said as Davis knocked and opened the door.

"It's Davis, Lois."

"I know," said Lois. "You're Jimmy Davis and we have known each other since middle school."

He didn't bother to correct the old woman. She was happy to see him and if it meant being a long lost friend to keep her that way, then so be it.

"How are you, Lois?" Davis asked the old woman.

"I've been thinking about you since you were here the last time. I could help you get to know some of the fossils around here. Help you get to know what they need."

"I don't know, Lois," Davis said, his voice heavy with trepidation.

"What's the worst that could happen?" Lois pleaded. "One sad, old broad might get a chance to have a little something to do around this goddamned prison, just once before she dies."

"I might lose my goddamned job," Davis barked.

"Not a chance, Jimmy," she soothed. The hope was rising in her voice. They can't keep anybody on the night shift, too much weird shit going on. All you've got to do is agree to stay on nights and bingo, you've got job security!"

Davis thought about it for a moment and agreed that there seemed to be very little chance of anything terrible happening by letting the old woman tag along with him and the nightshift seemed to have chosen him. Fighting fate like that seemed a little like tilting at windmills.

"Okay," said Davis "But if word of this gets out, I'll tell everyone you knocked me out and ran wild."

"Deal!" she said with glee.

They walked through the ward together, Lois talking his ear off and loving every minute of it and Davis pretending not to notice that she had told him the same stories six or seven times. They came to room 115 and Davis opened the door to go in and change the occupant.

"Where are you going?" asked Lois.

"I'm going in to change Mr. Grant."

"Arthur Grant, changed? Nonsense!" she blurted out. "Arthur Grant has had a colostomy since he came back from the war and hasn't worn a diaper in his whole goddamned adult life."

"Why would his name be in the book Nancy gave me, then?"

"Nancy Seasons is trying to make you look bad, trying to let you paint yourself into a corner. You keep doing stupid things like changing the wrong people and making all of us very unhappy and very complainy. We report you to the nurse, the nurse reports you to Nancy. Nancy says your job is on the line but that if you do her a small favour, it needn't be a permanent black mark on your record, yes? That'd be my guess."

"Lois?" Davis began.

"Uh-huh?" Lois replied.

"That's pretty specific."

"Jimmy, I am 88 years old. You don't make it this far without listening to things and figuring out that there are really only a couple types of people in this world and they are all the goddamned same. I have known all of the people that came here before you and they all let themselves be crushed under heel by Nancy Seasons' blustering and poisonous tongue. Most of them are in jail now."

"And the rest?" asked Davis, not really wanting to know.

"Dead, I should think," Lois said matter-of-factly.

"What does she want me for?" Davis asked glumly.

"It's not you, Jimmy. She's done this to so many others for so, so long. Let me see this book."

"You already made notes in it Lois," Davis explained. "The first night I met you."

"I did?" she asked sceptically.

Davis jogged back to the nurse's station and grabbed the black and white composition book from his backpack. He hurried back to Lois and showed it to her.

"What the hell is this?" Lois asked him. "This isn't even in English."

"What?" Davis asked incredulous.

"Look for yourself." Lois handed the book back to him.

Davis examined the page. It wasn't English and it wasn't what Nancy Seasons had given him before last shift.

The pages were full of a language Davis didn't recognize and along the margins were hand drawn symbols with pictograms. Davis stared at pictures of 15 people he didn't recognize. There were dates written on the bottoms of all the photos, ranging from 1910 to just two years ago. He assumed they were all dead and though he didn't know why, he knew with certainty they didn't die of old age.

Fascinated, he continued to flip through the book, which was full of the strange language and random translations of passages someone thought important enough to demystify. Until he came to the last few pages of the book that, when flipped upside down, revealed Nancy Season's instructions for the residents.

"What the hell is this?" Davis asked Lois, handing the book back to her.

"I don't know," she said after looking at the book for a time. "Nothing good ever came from a book with symbols and pictures of dead people in it. What I do know is you can't ever give this back to Nancy Seasons. If she doesn't know what this book is, she shouldn't ever find out. If she does already know then she's gonna come looking for this book and do something terrible with it. Either way, you need to get it as far away from her and this place as you can."

Davis opened the book again, on the inside cover were six names with 'MD' after each one. He assumed they were the former directors of Winterbourne. On the top of the first page was a small black cross with a backward letter 'c' coming out from the bottom of it. Written underneath of this symbol was a bold inscription. Davis tried to read it aloud.

"Yn awr yn dod I mi Marwolaeth mawr."

"Now what?" asked Lois.

"Sshh," Davis said, a little startled.

He was half expecting something to happen after the words left his mouth but guessed that, as knowledge in the darker arts was not one of his strong suits, nothing was going to and that suited him just fine.

"Lot of mumbo-jumbo," Lois spat. "Listen Jimmy, I'm going back to bed. You go check on Arthur Grant for me."

"I thought you said he didn't need to be changed?" He questioned.

"He doesn't," she said. "But he hasn't been looking well these last few days. He looked tired and frightened. Fear around this place is like mustard gas, it creeps slowly along the ground and kills silently. Look in on him, help him be strong."

His being strong seemed to be a recurring theme tonight.

"Okay, Lois," Davis promised. "I'll go after I take you back to your room."

"Go see to him now," she scolded him. "I can make my own way back to my room."

Davis did as he was told, but the thought of Nancy Seasons coming on the floor and asking why the old woman was not in her bed made his guts turn over. He supposed he would be all right if he went to Arthur Grant quickly and got back in time to escort Lois back to her room, imagining he could use the book for leverage if it came right down to it, but he hoped it wouldn't. The young man wasn't sure he was stubborn enough to do such a thing and Nancy Seasons scared him more than just a little.

Silently, he walked to Arthur Grant's room, number 129. It was the big corner one, normally reserved for double occupants but when Arthur's roommate had died the year before, they hadn't bothered to replace him. Davis didn't think this would last too much longer but in this place, he was beginning to find out, it didn't pay to second guess anything.

He opened the door and by the glow of the television, he could clearly see Arthur Grant lying on his bed. The old man looked up when the door open. A desiccated 'Hello' came from his general direction

"How are you doing Mr. Grant?" Davis asked nervously.

"Call me Arthur," he said. "Are you the new night man Lois was talking about, Jimmy, isn't it?"

"Umm...Davis, actually."

Arthur chuckled. "I thought something was a little off when she said the two of you dated in school. Heart of gold that old broad, but she's out of her bloody mind."

He was a large man, even lying down. The bed sheets covered him from the waist down but despite the thin white hair on his head and the oxygen hose trailing from his nose, he looked remarkably strong even now. His thick working man's hands held onto the blanket's edge.

Davis laughed with the old man. It felt good—he couldn't remember the last time he laughed and it was nice to do it again.

"She's worried about you," Davis began, "she asked me to look in on you but if you're okay, I'll go make sure she gets back to her room."

"Actually," Arthur said quietly, "could you stay for a moment?"

"Sure," said Davis. "What can I do for you?"

"Just sit with me for a bit, would you?"

They sat in silence for a time, Arthur watched TV and Davis tried not to feel uncomfortable. Davis resolved to break the silence and excuse himself. He did, after all, have work to do and took a deep, purposeful breath as Arthur began to speak.

"I'm so frightened," Arthur said.

"Of what?" Davis asked innocently.

"My time is up, son. I can feel it. It's crushing me, like a stone slab on my chest," Arthur began. A heavy sigh left his lips. Davis could sense that he was searching for what to say next.

"I spent my whole life," Arthur lamented, "Working for somebody else. Always chasing the promise of more money, busting my body and selling my soul to get more. I never married, never had children. There were women, sure, even one or two I could have stayed with and loved but I didn't. It isn't any disease that left me like this, greed and my own stupidity has crippled my body and left me empty. I am going to hell because I refused to see the world farther than the end of my nose." A single tear rolled across the wrinkled, mottled cheek.

Davis wasn't sure what to say to the old man and fumbled to comfort him.

"Arthur, I-"

"You don't have to say anything, son," Arthur said. "Just stay with me. I don't want to be alone."

Davis could hear the old man's breath become slower and start to rattle in his throat like chunks of coal rushing down a tin shoot. He could hear the sadness in his voice and feel tears welling up in his eyes.

"I'll stay as long as you need me to."

He reached over, took Arthur's hand and noticed how cold and unnatural it felt. Like holding a glove packed tight with snow. He gave it a squeeze and the cold hand squeezed back. Davis looked up at the old man's face and saw the grey eyes were half open, and feared Arthur had already passed.

"Arthur?" Davis called out to him.

"Yes?" Arthur replied, his eyes not moving.

"Nothing."

"Davis?" Arthur asked. "Davis can you hold my hand?"

Davis swallowed and knew the end was just around the corner.

"I am holding your hand, Arthur." Davis fought back tears. "I'm right here."

He squeezed the old man's hand but received no reply. Arthur's breath became laboured and Davis closed his eyes.

"I'm so scared," Arthur gasped.

"I'm right here," Davis comforted him.

Davis bent and kissed the old man on the forehead—he felt as if on fire.

"I'm right here, Arthur." He squeezed the old man's hand again. "I'm not going anywhere."

Davis heard a rumble and thought he imagined it. Grief played tricks with his mind but when he saw the bright golden light coming from behind the closet door he knew it wasn't a dream. The metal handle turned and the door cracked open bathing Arthur's face in a golden, near mystical glow. Davis wanted to get up, feeling he owed the golden light some kind of reverence, but he told the old man that he would be here to the end and, though he was many things, a liar wasn't chief among them. So he stayed seated, holding Arthur Grant's hand.

As the door inched open further, he stood up, knocking over his chair. He still held Arthur's hand as he balled his other one into a fist. Davis felt himself seethe with indignation at the thought of those heinous things tearing this scared and lonely old man to shreds. He looked around the room for something to use as a weapon and found an 18-inch plastic shoe horn lying beside Arthur's bed. The younger man raised it, sword like, above his head brandishing it as grievously as possible.

"Come out of there you ugly bastard!" Davis demanded.

The door swung open and Davis stood in awe of what emerged from the closet. It was not much bigger than the reptilian ape thing he had seen with Mrs. K. Nesbit, but what Davis beheld wasn't unnerving in the least. Davis fell to his knees, humbled by the majesty of what he saw.

It was a small boy, the most beautiful child Davis thought he had ever seen. Delicate black feathered wings extended up from the center of his slight, muscular back and he wore a humble white, thigh-length tunic. Around his waist was a fine, shiny, black leather belt which hung a short, lustrous sword. He stepped into the room and took in his surroundings. The boy met Davis' gaze and gave him a heartfelt smile that was so pure, so imbued with love and flawless ardor that Davis turned away from him ashamed, as though he wasn't worthy of looking at this exquisite little being.

The winged child crossed the room gracefully and took Arthur's hand from Davis. He rubbed his elegant, small hand from one side of the old man's temple, across his eyes and stopped after reaching the other side. Davis felt like the light in the room dimmed and knew Arthur was gone. The beautiful child looked at Davis, smiled his perfect smile again and said, "You stayed with him."

The child's voice was a confounding and awesome thing to hear, so perfect in its clarity and timber that Davis thought his ears were being crushed by the magnificent, overwhelming sound.

"I promised him I would stay," Davis answered.

"Many would not have stayed," said the winged child.

"He was alone and afraid. I told him I wouldn't let him go out that way."

"Though you knew he would die whether you stayed or not?" the perfect boy asked him.

"Because I knew it," Davis retorted.

The small winged being walked over to Davis and took his hand.

"You have a strength that few possess, and those without such strength will seek you out," the child said. "Have you the will to defend them as you were willing to fight for this man?"

"Yes," Davis said, surprised by how quickly and surely he answered.

The winged child pulled on Davis' hand with such incredible strength, that he was forced to bend to face its own unpretentious level. The angelic boy drew him in and kissed his forehead. Staring knowingly into the young man's eyes before releasing his hand.

"You are worthy of the duty laid before you. You will bring peace to many should you embrace the mantle," said the child. He walked back into the closet and disappeared, taking the radiant golden light with him.

Davis felt the sting of thick tears running down his face; the tears of someone who had laboured under the illusion of having known love for a whole lifetime, only to see true love, real love as the chair is kicked from underneath his feet. He pulled up the bedclothes and covered Arthur's face. The younger man could feel his hand tremble with uncertainty, holding it above Arthur before laying it on the dead man's forehead. He walked to the bathroom, turned on the light and splashed a generous amount of cold water on his face. Then Davis dropped to his knees, thought of the cold, lifeless giant man in the bed in the middle of the room and wept like an abandoned child.

Jenn looked away from the monitor and toward the man in the comfortable tan and red ski sweater.

"It is him," she said.

CHAPTER 11

Nancy Seasons lay awake in her king-sized bed. She couldn't sleep, unlike her present companion who snored away happily. Her mind was far too busy to let her body go to sleep. She brought home the young orderly as a diversion, a plaything, and now she was bored with him, wanted him gone. A casually aimed arm nudged him. He grunted an objection and rolled slightly. When she elbowed him sharply in the ribs he received the message, loud and clear.

"What?" he croaked hoarsely.

"Get out," she said calmly.

"What?" he replied, incredulously.

"Get out!" she screamed an abnormal, cornered-animal wail and it scared the hell out of him

He fumbled for his clothes, dressed as quickly as he could and ran for the front door.

Nancy smiled a little and got up out of her bed. She laid awake all night re-reading the director's letter in her mind. Absentmindedly, she gave the book to the new nightshift man but was confident she could get it back. She planned to make him one of the 12, after all. He was a good-looking kid, so just doing away with him just wouldn't do. Why not have a bit of fun first? Invite him to the house and use him like a bouncy castle. Maybe slip something into his drink or perhaps she would just hit him over the head, but something to make sure he was incapacitated long before she trussed him up. Then she would make his fear reach fever pitch.

"I'll cut his goddamned heart out and eat it in front of him," Nancy said.

Getting the book back after that posed no problem. What did, however, was finding the heir—Death's successor. Nancy never heard of something so outlandish. Death didn't have an heir, Death was eternal and unfaltering—Death just was. The director never lied to her, though. He was far too meek for deception this grand. Especially for the promise of power this great. The director was never power-hungry enough to perform this ritual in its entirety, but he knew Nancy had enough zeal to do it. She was confident that if the director said Death had a successor, then it was absolutely so.

Nancy walked downstairs to her library and studied the rows of books the director had left her. After careful examination, she pulled one or two off the shelves and began to comb through the pages, looking for some morsel that would tell her how to spot Death's only scion. Her thoughts went back to her first meeting with the director and how he took her under his wing and set her on this dark path all those years ago. How he taught her all about the evil arts and how, when he died, he left all of the contents of his secret library to her. She was grateful and excited to gain power using the knowledge he had given her, but when it came right down to it, all of this nefarious witchy stuff was more reading than devilry and overall, a lot of frigging work. She breathed a sigh and was just about to close the book when she found it.

The ancient manuscript read:

> It was Edmund the Mad who first discovered that Death, in the classical sense, was an office rather than a single living (immortal) entity. Death, or the Servant of the Void, is the chief emissary of Thanatos, the Omega. Death will retain his post until such time as the passing of one thousand years or when acted upon by an external arcane influence.

> Before the passing of one thousand years, Death must choose a scion to inherit the office. It would likely be an orphan of questionable parentage with few or no remaining ties to anyone. Someone for whom a thousand years of service would be of no consequence.

> If a successor is not named or the process of relinquishing the office were to be interrupted, a divergence would begin in the balance between the living and the dead, one that could only be rectified by a cataclysm the like of which has never been seen in the world of man. In addition, the outgoing Servant of the Void would be subject to torment and misery until the end of time.

Nancy Seasons set down the antiquated volume and smiled as she rose. From the briefcase beside her nightstand, she took out a stack of papers with a photograph of Davis Mareth. She liked to investigate her employees thoroughly, mostly illegally. Especially if she intended to make a sacrifice of them. She read his file intently and she thought pumping the young archivist from the public records department for more than just information had turned out to be a good thing for both of them. He didn't have a problem bringing her the history of everyone she asked for and she, in turn, didn't have a problem introducing him to the upper echelon of Winterbourne's political world.

She looked over Davis' file. Orphaned at birth by his mother's death in an automobile accident and the identity of his father was listed as unknown. He became a ward of the court and put in the orphanage system where he bounced around until he was old enough to leave. He disappeared from the area for a number of years and then returned and entered school. Shortly after graduating, he secured the job at Winterbourne and the rest was history.

"Jesus," Nancy exclaimed. "He should just wear a sign saying he is an excellent candidate to be your new Death."

She decided she would make him suffer like no other. "He will beg me for release," she said. "And I will dangle it in front of him like a carrot on a stick. Then I will show him what real power is."

CHAPTER 12

"Lydia Beckett, come on down!" said the voice on the television, but Ezra Schneider wasn't listening. He looked at the pack of cigarettes lying on the TV table and took one out. The man dug around his pockets and came out with a solitary wooden match and striking it against his filthy thumbnail, lit the Chesterfield.

"You goddamned ass bag!" he shouted to the empty room.

Ezra looked old; the yellowed white hair that covered his head and chin cemented that, even if his behaviour didn't. He took a folded picture from his pocket and stared at it for the longest time, stopping occasionally to pinch his nostrils and wipe away the snot and tears. The image was of a plain-looking woman and a beautiful, little blonde-haired girl.

"Goddammit," he said.

"Lydia Beckett, how much would you pay for this gorgeous washer and dryer suite? One thousand dollars? Fifteen hundred dollars?"

He held up the picture and pressed it to his lips.

"I'm so sorry," he sobbed and threw the picture across the room. The old man covered his face and tried to not look at the picture lying on the floor. Ezra stood and tried to walk into the kitchen, stopping on the way to pick up the photo and clutch it to his chest before he once again took his place on the chair in front of the television.

"Lydia, what if we were to take that washer and dryer and add a color television?"

The man thought back to the good times he had with them, the times when he threw the child so high in the air, the woman thought she might never come down. And how they all laughed when the man caught the child in his arms and kissed her like she might disappear in an instant if he didn't.

"Kimberly Boseman, come on down!" the television blared.

"Fuck," said the man. "Fuck, fuck, fuck, fuck this, fuck me and FUCK YOU!"

The man stood up and walked toward the landing by the stairs. He walked into the kitchen and opened the cupboard beside the refrigerator, taking the nickel-plated .38 revolver from inside the cupboard and headed back to the living room. Ezra sat in a barcalounger, cocked the pistol then put the barrel in his mouth. As he looked at the picture of the woman and the little girl for a second time, he felt the cold nickel against his teeth and his finger moved closer to the trigger.

"Jeannie Campbell, come on down!"

He took a deep breath and closed his eyes. The old man saw the little girl run toward him and ask,

"Daddy, did I tell you I loved you today?"

He squeezed his eyes shut and felt warm tears roll down his face.

"Give me a kiss, Daddy," the little blonde-haired girl said.

The man opened his eyes and squeezed the trigger. The pistol discharged and all was black and silent.

Nancy Seasons took the pistol from the old man's hands and knelt down beside him.

"Ezra, it doesn't work that way."

"What in the thumping hell are you doing here, you harpy."

"I am here to help you."

"Oh, absolutely," Ezra said sarcastically. "You can help me up off of this floor and then you can help your greasy, fat ass out that bastarding door."

"Oh, okay," Nancy said coolly. "If you don't want to hear what I have to say, I will go, but I told you many years ago that if anybody could find the answer to your problem, I could."

She turned to leave and Ezra quickly stood between her and the door.

"What are you jabber boxing about?"

Nancy pulled a chair away from the kitchen table and slowly sat down, never once taking her eyes off of him. She languidly opened her handbag and took out the manila file folder that was stuffed with papers.

"Now look it fuck-sock," Ezra spat. "You either tell me what you're on about or leave me alone. I don't have time for all this hocus pocus bullshit."

"No Ezra," she began. "No hocus pocus. Well, beyond what we are already doing. I mean, I *am* talking to a man who is 115 years old, yes?"

"I'm listening," Ezra growled.

"What if I told you I could send you to your daughter?"

"You better watch your bastarding mouth or you'll get it smacked. My daughter is deader than Elvis and nothing anybody does is going to change that. I was trying to go see her when you barged in here."

"No," Nancy said, her shrill voice stabbing at his ears. "You're not listening. I said I could send you to be with your daughter. I know perfectly well that she is dead, Ezra Schneider, and I know that the shame of what you did likely drove her to it. I also know exactly how to send you to her."

Ezra sat down in the chair across the table from Nancy and studied her face carefully. If being alive as long as he taught him anything, it was how to read someone and tell if they were yanking your chain. Nancy Seasons was either a master of complete deception or she was telling the truth.

"All right, you have my attention. How in the hell do you propose to do this?"

"Hell," Nancy said, opening the file folder, "has nothing at all to do with it."

She pushed the file folder toward him, a picture of Davis Mareth on top of the papers. Ezra pushed the picture aside and picked up the top sheet of paper.

"What does an orphan have to do with my daughter?"

"It's not whose child he is not," Nancy said cryptically, "but whose child he is going to be."

"What in the holy blue fuck does that even mean?" Ezra asked. "I told you I wasn't interested in any of your spooky hokum."

"It means," she said, looking directly into his soul, "that you and this orphan will soon both be very dead."

CHAPTER 13

"What did you just say?" Davis asked.

"I know it's a lot to take in all at once," Jenn told him.

"A lot to take in? The fucking Hindenburg crash was a lot to take in. Katy Russell taking off her sun dress and standing in front of me when we played Spin the Bottle in the third grade was a lot to take in. This is, this is…" he gasped, fumbling for the right words. "I need some air."

Davis stood to leave the nurse's station and didn't get far. His legs turned to rubber and the room spun. He groped for something to steady himself and found the door way a willing helper but in steadying himself he only served to give the nausea rising in the pit of his stomach room to move. Instantly he felt the hot, sour liquid rush up his throat and fire out his mouth. Mercifully, he hadn't had anything to eat apart from a cup of watery coffee and a bowl of the cafeteria's famous no-flavour soup. The vomiting soon gave way to dry heaves. His body stopped the spasms and he blacked out entirely. When he came to, his head was in Jenn's lap and she mopped his brow with a cool, damp cloth.

"Hi," she said softly.

He tried to sit up but she pulled him down.

"Just keep still for a bit," Jenn whispered. She bent over and kissed him tenderly on the forehead, her hair tickled across his face. Davis thought she looked very different upside down. Not unpleasant, far from it, just not at all like herself. Her lap was warm and he felt so comfortable staying there that he didn't care if he ever left it again. At that moment he knew he was in love with her. He leaned up to her and tried to kiss her lips.

"You've got puke breath." She laughed. "And I'm dead."

He forced himself off her lap and sat up, just looking at her. She was glowing, though he couldn't be sure that he wasn't still a little dizzy.

"Tell me again," Davis asked.

Jenn took a deep breath and let it out slowly.

"You are the heir," she said.

"Whose heir?" he asked her again.

"You are the Mortal Scion, the successor to the Servant of The Void, Agent of the Omega, the True and Everlasting Terminus, the Ayatollah of No Moreover, the one, the only, Death."

"How did I get to be so lucky?" Davis asked, trying not to dry heave.

She asked him a question instead.

"What do you remember about your parents?"

"I never knew them," he began, the barely concealed bitterness coming through the words. "They gave me up for adoption the day I was born."

"What if I told you your parents didn't give you up? What if I said you were the most important thing to your mother and that she willingly, gladly gave her life for you?"

"I would say you are sadly mistaken," Davis challenged. "My mother was young and buggered up and gave me away almost as soon as she pushed me out."

"No," Jenn said sympathetically. "I wish I could tell you that was true. Your mother was very young, yes, and she had her problems, but she loved you and loved the idea of being your mother. It gave her life focus. She died on the day you were born and willingly offered to give her life for you. You were the one good thing she did and she died finally realizing that."

Davis sat silently and said nothing for a while. He looked to Jenn with eyes that were nearly crimson and half closed from the sadness and exhaustion swirling around his head.

"I haven't got much on him," Jenn replied.

"Gimme what you got."

"He was a man your mother met at a party."

"That's the lot?" he asked in disbelief.

"I'm afraid so. Look, I told you it wasn't much."

"It isn't anything," Davis snorted.

Jenn smiled at him, the look of someone who has just delivered a wrapped package to a friend, knowing that in a moment or two, it would be the best gift they have ever received.

"Every thousand years or so, the big D has enough of his job and decides to retire. He names a successor and off he goes to die somewhere nice and warm. Tahiti has always been popular. The successor steps up and assumes the mantle—that's the robe and the scythe—and all is right and natural with the world."

"What happens if there is no successor?"

"What?" Jenn squawked.

"Like if nobody could be found or if someone was found but didn't want the job?"

"There is always a successor, but if he were to refuse…" She muttered to herself for an awkward moment.

"Jenn?" Davis asked, bringing her back to reality.

"Huh?" she asked.

"What would happen?"

"There are only two things I know of that could hinder the succession. If the heir refuses to take the cloak and the scythe, and to my knowledge that only happened once and it was very brief. Or if somebody was fool enough to try the ritual."

"Well of course there's a ritual," Davis said, refusing to hide his sarcasm.

"There's always a ritual."

"That's part of the problem," Jenn said. "There is always a ritual. Humans are never satisfied that things are black and white."

"What do you mean?" Davis asked.

"I mean that it is all very simple. We are born, we grow and get to experience tons of amazing things that no other human being will ever experience the way you will. Your experience is totally subjective and independent of anyone else's. Then we grow old, our bodies grow old and weak and then we die. It is a simple equation, but nobody is ever happy with that. They always want more—more money, more sex, more booze and drugs, more life."

"What's wrong with wanting more?"

"Because there isn't any more." Jenn was beginning to shout. "There doesn't need to be any more. We started inventing gods and happy places to fool ourselves into thinking there is more, but we've already got everything we need right here."

"How does a ritual fit into all of this?" Davis asked, trying to get her mind away from the angry gear it was heading toward.

"A long time ago—nobody's certain when—some foolish old man figured out a loophole. He figured out that Death is a job like any other and if you can force your way into the position, you can start to change the rules. You could remake the rules of life and death itself."

"Why would anyone want to do that?" Davis asked her.

"You really aren't getting this, are you?" She took a deep breath and Davis could tell her mood was settling a little.

"Eternal life for anyone you wanted or instant death to anybody that got in your way, what's not to like?"

"If that's the case," he began, "why wouldn't somebody be foolish enough to say it?"

"What everyone who ever tried the damn thing failed to realize, is how important the balance is and just what a monstrous amount of power and responsibility the job carries. Even an hour of The Omega not operating as it is supposed to and the balance between life and death gets massively out of whack."

Davis stared at her blankly. He wanted to know what she was talking about but he didn't. On the surface, he got the concept but she was getting deeper and more in depth and he feared his brain would leave the conversation altogether.

"Okay look," she started again. "All of us are born with something to do, some greater purpose. Maybe you will cure cancer or maybe you will assassinate the president. Maybe you'll have a couple of kids and propagate the species just a little bit more. Whatever it is, once you have done what you're meant to, the hourglass is turned and you need to start saying your goodbyes."

"You die right after you've done your thing?"

"Almost never," she said. "But you could. You could go on to live a long and personally meaningful existence or you could step off a curb and get flattened by a bus. The rules were meant to get people to appreciate what they had. I'm wandering away from what I was saying now, but once your purpose is fulfilled, you're number is free to come up. It's completely random, but still, it keeps the scales even."

Davis listened more intently now, nodding as though she said something he finally understood and all the other things were falling into place.

"Now," she said with a good deal of relief. "What would happen if there were no one around to usher out the people with numbers that came up?"

"Do you mean…" Davis began with some hesitation.

"No, not zombies," Jenn said as though reading his mind. "The dead wouldn't die and there would be nothing anybody could do until a new, proper Death was put back into place. Then something gigantic would have to happen in order to restore the balance again. Some massive loss of life to get all of the not-dead's back where they needed to be."

"Has that ever happened?" Davis asked quietly.

"World War I, World War II, the Hindenburg, The Great Chicago Fire. It's happened more than you think and it still isn't at equilibrium."

Davis was full of questions but remained silent for a time, thinking of the best one to ask first.

"Are you…Death?" he asked her.

He regretted the question the second it left his lips. What he really wanted to ask her was what she was doing for dinner, if she even ate, or if she wanted a beer or maybe to go to his place. He could scarcely focus on anything but his desire to be with this woman and it was serving to distract him from everything else.

"No," she said flatly. "I am not."

The tone of her voice forced him to think of something else quickly. "What do you know about this ritual thing?"

"I've heard some things," she said. "Rumours mostly. It involves the killing of 12 innocent people. Twelve people who have lived virtuous lives and have brought no harm on any other person. After that, there are words and candles and ancient drawings. Hundreds of people have tried it since the loophole was discovered, the last person to try it was the director here, the man who came after the one that killed me—who also tried it incidentally. It would probably be written down in a book of some kind, though not necessarily. It wouldn't be in any language you couldn't possibly read or speak and it would be full of diagrams and drawings."

He beamed at her.

"What?" she asked slightly embarrassed.

"Nothing, not a thing."

"I guess I knew a little more than I let on," she said, feeling her cheeks flush.

There are moments in one's life when it dawns on you that the answer just looked you right in the face and gave you a big, sloppy kiss. There are other times when you have the answer, have had the answer all along and present it to someone who promptly says you couldn't be more wrong if your hair was on backward.

"Would it be in a book like this?" Davis held up the black and white composition book.

"No," she said. "My guess is it would be a large, leather-bound, dusty, ancient looking thing."

"Oh." Davis felt slightly affronted. "My mistake."

He flipped the book open to the front page and murdered the first passage for a second time.

"Yn awr yn dod I mi Marwolaeth mawr."

Jenn snapped her head around to look at him. "What did you just say?"

"Something in a language I couldn't possibly read or speak."

Jenn stared at Davis with wide eyes and mouth open.

"What?" Davis asked when she continued to stare at him.

"Ask me again sometime," she said. "Let me look at that book, will you?"

Jenn slowly flipped the pages of the composition book and considered each one, carefully studying the words and symbols on each page and looking for the answers she was pretty sure she already had.

"Where did you get this book?" she asked him.

"Nancy Seasons gave it to me the night I started here. There's a list of residents on the back page. I don't think she knew what it was. Nobody could be stupid enough to give away a book as valuable as that, could they?"

"I don't know," Jenn said in a serious tone. "She's up to something and I don't imagine it's in any way good. You need to stay away from her; we need to get you off of the night shift for a day or two. She'll think you're still on that shift and come looking for you then."

"How do you propose to do that?" Davis groaned. "Nancy Seasons does all the scheduling around here."

"She's not the only one who can use a computer," Jenn said. "Being dead has its advantages. When she figures out where you are, she'll believe she sent you there."

"Sounds like fun. I've never worked on any other shift before," said Davis. "I don't know anybody."

"They're a good bunch," she reassured him. "Besides, you have Lois. She wouldn't let anybody hurt you, Jimmy."

She started to walk out the double doors to the hallway then stopped and turned to him.

"This is serious, Davis. I want you to think about everything you heard tonight, I know it's a lot to digest but it's important that you make the right decision. And no matter what you do, you cannot let Nancy Seasons get that book. She might not know what it is yet, but when she does, she'll come looking for it and if she figures out how to use it, we're all screwed."

CHAPTER 14

"**Y**ou want to kill this guy over a book?" Ezra Schneider said.

"Well…yes," said Nancy, "and no."

"Can I get you a warm up?" the pretty young waitress asked Ezra.

Ezra nodded silently and the waitress filled his cup without looking at him then scurried off to help someone locate their missing eggs. Nancy stood then sat down beside him.

"What the balls are you doing?" he snarled.

She leaned into him and whispered. "I don't want anyone to hear any of this."

"Nobody in this place gives a good goddamn what anybody else is saying. They are all too concerned with how shitty their own lives are to worry about how shitty anybody else's is."

"Really?" Nancy asked a little surprised at his answer.

"Really," he said. "Watch."

Ezra Schneider stood up, dropped his pants, and began to shout at the top of his lungs.

"I am a fuzzy, four-legged Fazoo. I have a book that will give me the power over death himself. All of you should tremble and kneel down before me. I am your lord and master now!"

A few scattered heads looked up from their breakfasts and some even began to whisper, but the reaction was lukewarm at best. It didn't even garner a wagging finger from the restaurant's manager.

"See?" he said defiantly. "Now get back to the other side of the bastarding table."

Nancy shuffled back to the other side and leaned in to him, heedless of his earlier demonstration.

"Now, as I was about to say…"

"And holy Jesus woman," Ezra barked, cutting her off. "Your breath smells like Satan's asshole. Do you not own a toothbrush?"

Nancy Seasons cleared her throat, collected herself and stood up. She crossed the restaurant and opened the front door.

"Where are you going?" Ezra called after her.

"I don't need you, Mr. Schneider. I offered to help you but you obviously aren't interested in what I have to say. I'll just be on my way then."

He sat at the table, hoping desperately to call her bluff. The truth was that if she told the truth about the book, she could help him leave this life at last. He sucked in a deep breath and whatever pride he had left and stood up.

"Wait, Nancy," he said through gritted teeth. "Please."

The smile that crept onto her lips said she had him over a barrel and he knew it. She walked slowly and deliberately back to the table, her eyes boring a hole through the center of his head as she sat down.

"I can help you, Ezra, but you will do exactly as you are told. If you don't, I will guarantee that you will have all of eternity to ponder your daughter's fate as you eat bullet after bullet, knowing for certain that you are as big a failure now as you were when she was still alive."

"I could snap your neck without thinking twice," Ezra hissed.

"And I could walk out right now," Nancy retorted. "Either way, you're damned to wander."

"I'm listening," Ezra said.

The old man put his head down on the table and growled softly in bristling compliance as she explained to him about Davis Mareth and the book and what it all meant. He'd been in this situation once before, backed into a corner by someone using the weight of his own conscience against him. It made him angry and dangerous, like a dog that's been hit too many times. Backing down if you faced it head on but if you turned your back on it, it would bury its fangs in your leg the first chance it got.

"First thing we need to do is get the book. Mareth works the night shift and tends to sleep in the Nurse's station. It shouldn't be too difficult to get it from him. Even for you."

Her words were dripping with poison and she meant to humiliate him. She held the rest of his time in the palm of her hand and in the end he would categorically know who his master was.

"Ugnh," he grunted his compliance with her statement.

"He must not be killed, not right away anyway, and not by you. When the time comes, I must be the one to strike the final blow. It will be your job to keep me safe from harm, once everything has started, I will be completely vulnerable until I have assumed the power of The Void."

Ezra perked up after hearing that.

"Completely vulnerable, eh?" he asked, curiosity piqued.

"Don't get any ideas," she admonished him. "If I die in the middle of the ritual, you will continue your pathetic half-existence on this planet until time runs out. I am the only one who can help you now, remember that."

"Ugnh," Ezra grunted again.

She got up to leave and leaned over him.

"I'll be in touch; I'm off now to find a toothbrush." She stood to leave and a thought popped into her head. She slowly bent down and leaned toward him, as though she might kiss him.

"I own you," she breathed in his ear and then stood to face him. "If you try to betray me, I promise you the last 88 years will seem like a walk on a Sunday afternoon compared to the exquisite misery you will feel until the end of time."

She blew a final, rank breath in his face and walked out the front door. The old man covered his nose in half-mocking disgust and watched Nancy until the door closed after her.

Ezra Schneider sat alone at the table and took a long pull from his cold cup of coffee. He took the crumpled, faded picture from his pocket and looked lovingly at it. A teary smile danced across his lips. The little blonde girl's face bore a serious expression, furrowed brow and pursed lips. The photographer had merely suggested something other than a toothless grin and it was a close as she could manage. Though it betrayed her real personality, Ezra could remember the full belly laughter that erupted from her when he would chase her around the backyard. In and out of the clean sheets hanging on the line, and how the girl's mother would yell at both of them to settle down before she wound up choking and sputtering on the lawn. The little girl would beg him not to stop and he always explain that her mother was right, just before he would chase her again.

He pressed the picture to his lips and kissed the image.

"Soon baby, soon. Daddy just has to do one more thing and then he'll be right back."

They were the last words he ever spoke to her.

He had been called into his supervisor's office the day before with instructions to go and see the director and not to ask any questions. In a time when not doing as your superiors asked could mean the difference between your family eating well or having to beg for handouts from the neighbours, Ezra Schneider kept his head down and pretended he didn't know what was really happening around him.

At first he was asked to dispose of bundles—large, heavy ones that were the length of a rolled up area rug with the basic shape of a human being. He supposed they were bodies of the people who died while at Winterbourne but really didn't care to know the truth. Ezra would pick them up from a cold dark room in the western-most corner of the building's lower floor then transport them by means of a wheeled garbage cart to the far eastern corner of Winterbourne's basement to the incinerator. It was said that the fires of the incinerator were hot enough to wither a body to ash. When Ezra burned the first of the large bundles, he was pretty certain that was precisely what he was doing. There were 10 such bundles he had been asked to quietly dispose of, one on the second Tuesday of every month. On being told of an eleventh bundle, Ezra was given a note by the director which read:

> Your work has been exceptional thus far, Mr. Schneider.
> Please report to my office in one month's time. I have one

more thing to ask of you. If you perform this small task with the same degree of excellence and professionalism you have shown thus far, your wife and child will want for nothing as long as they live.

Ezra remembered his heart pounding with excitement, thinking of the joy that would shine in his daughter's eyes after learning she would never have to worry about ever feeling bad or gasping for breath again. And the look on his wife's face when they walked up the stairs to their new house. All bought and paid for because the director knew how to reward loyalty and silence. He smiled to himself and tried to reason that if it were bodies he was disposing of, they were the bodies of the lunatics who died naturally or during the procedures the good doctors of Winterbourne were using to help these poor unfortunates.

The week went by and the second Tuesday arrived without much incident. Ezra dutifully walked to the cold room in the west corner but there was no rug length bundle for him to get rid of. The old man didn't understand and took the director's note from his pocket and read it over again then cursed himself as stupid for not going to the man's office as the note had asked him to do. He reasoned there couldn't be a bundle in there with him; if they were what he suspected they were it would draw far too much leery conversation from the rest of the staff.

When he walked into the office, the director sat behind his large oak desk, reading from a massive, antiquated looking book.

"Ah Mr. Schneider," said the director. "I am delighted you have decided to do me this one last favour."

"Certainly, sir," Ezra said. "Anything to help."

"That's the spirit."

The director stood and beckoned Ezra to follow him. Ezra trailed behind him cautiously. He had an uneasy feeling about what was going to happen, and a feeling he was powerless to do anything about it. The old orderly put a hand into the pocket of his hospital whites and felt for the picture. Ezra's thoughts remained firmly on her as he followed the director through a set of doors and on to dark corridor to the south of the director's office. He had never been down here before and wasn't certain how they got down there. He thought his hopes of a quick getaway, if he needed one, were fading with every step he took.

When they finally came to the small room, the director allowed Ezra to enter first. The room was barren save for sheets of dirty tarpaulin covering the floor and walls. In the middle of the room sitting on top of one of the sheets of tarpaulin was a high-backed wooden arm chair, and tied to that chair was a pretty, full-figured young nurse with dark hair.

"What the fuck is this?" Ezra said, still in complete shock at seeing the bound woman.

The director pulled one of the tarps off of the wall.

"Look out that window and tell me what you see" he told Ezra.

Ezra stepped up to the window where he could see a small blonde haired girl running back and forth with two of the other orderlies. The three of them were far enough away that he couldn't be certain it was his daughter, but the feeling in the pit of his stomach told him it was. The two orderlies both towered over the little girl and she could almost run between their legs. The director waved out the window to the two men and one waved back.

"With another wave from me, they'll snap her neck like a piece of kindling."

Ezra motioned toward the director, contemplating whether or not he could cross the small room quickly enough to get to the man before he could raise his hands. Getting himself, his daughter and this dark-haired woman out of harm's way without too much interference.

"Do you actually think you can move on me faster than I can wave my hand?" he chuckled.

Ezra knew he couldn't and dropped his head in defeat.

"Now that I have your complete attention, you will do exactly as you are told or you will carry your child home in a pine box."

"How do I know that's even my girl?" Ezra asked defiantly.

"Are you willing to take that chance? Move closer, let's find out."

"What is it you want?" Ezra asked.

"This woman," sighed the director, "was to be part of a much larger picture, but her desire to involve my wife in the dalliances she and I have shared, has left me with no alternative but to make her the last of an even dozen souls whose deaths will assure me of a power you could not possibly imagine. Think of it as taking a life to spare the life of your child. An eye for an eye, if you will."

Ezra fell to his knees, tears of anger and hopelessness burning his face.

No!" he shouted. "I cannot do this. Anything but this. I could give you money, I could take my family and go away and I could swear to keep your secret until the day I die."

"No," said the director. "I think not. You are too clever not to go to the authorities with what you know and I would spend the rest of my very short life dancing at the end of a rope. No, the only way to keep you quiet is to make you as guilty in all of this as I am. Now get on with it."

Ezra suddenly became aware that the dark-haired woman had been completely silent up to this point. He thought perhaps the director had given her something.

"Is she doped?" Ezra asked.

"She had two or three glasses of brandy, to calm her nerves," the director said dismissively.

Ezra looked around the walls and noticed a length of rope hanging from one of the pieces of tarpaulin, took his pocket knife out and proceeded to cut off a three foot piece. He stood behind the woman and slowly raised the rope to the back of her head.

"I'll leave you to it," the director hissed as he walked out of the small room.

Ezra looked out the window again and saw the blonde haired girl running with the two large men.

"I'm so sorry," he said to the woman. His heart cried out.

The woman gave no reply and Ezra thought for a moment that she might already be dead. He lowered the rope, placed his hand against the woman's cheek and felt the warmth of her skin. She was still very much alive and under the influence of something stronger than a few glasses of brandy. Her head sagged forward after touching her cheek. His right hand let go of the rope, and for a moment he thought about walking around to face her.

"I'm sorry," he said to her lolling head. "I'm so, so sorry. Please, I don't want to do this." He could feel his eyes beginning to well up.

"Please," he begged. "Please open your eyes and I swear we'll all go home. All of us together. Please!" He sobbed at the dark-haired woman as he paced behind her.

Ezra Schneider thought again of his child and the newfound health and security his actions would bring her, while visions of her horror and disgust after learning what he had done to get it frolicked mockingly in his head. He knew that his life would never be the same either way, and he would carry the guilt of it, like a scar on his soul, for the rest of his days. With no alternative he closed his eyes, put the garrotte around the woman's neck and pulled for all he was worth.

The old man opened his eyes. He was certain it was finished. The director stood over top of him and the dead woman. He was flanked by the two orderlies he had seen outside, one of whom was carrying a little blonde haired girl who was not his daughter but one of the children from the east wing of Winterbourne Home.

"Well done, Ezra," the director gloated. "Thank you for that."

"You bastard fuck!" Ezra shouted and lunged at the man.

He felt the straight right, ham fist of one of the orderlies' crash into his nose and in an instant, all went black.

 CHAPTER 15

David Mareth wandered into the halls of Winterbourne home at 5:45 the next morning. He felt like he was walking in a dream, slightly out of place and more than a little confused. If the night shift was a little odd, working on the day shift was downright alien.

"Jimmy!" Lois waved and jumped up and down. Truthfully, it was more of a laboured bend at the knees and a slow rise back up, but she was excited to see him.

"Lois!" Davis called back.

He wanted to hug her but thought better of it, not because there was any sort of awkwardness about it but because he was afraid of playing favourites on a shift he was unfamiliar with. The young man decided it was worth the risk, walked over then gave her a friendly embrace.

"Davis," called out another orderly. "Come with me."

They walked down the hallway from the nurse's station, pushing a rolling cart piled high with towels and sheets and the various kinds of soaps and creams they use to get the elderly residents up and ready for the day. He thought it strange being on this shift, walking around in the light of day and actually seeing people awake.

Having a few weeks of working on the night shift under his belt already, Davis was comfortable with the routines of the job. His nights usually consisted of changing a few wet briefs, chasing some wandering seniors and trying desperately to stay awake. The latter of which, he was less than successful at but he didn't have to interact with anyone. Not that he was opposed to it; he simply wasn't sure how to do it. When they're sleeping, seniors don't tend to tell you they don't like the gray sweater you've picked out or their toothbrush is hurting their eyes. They snore away contentedly and grunt occasionally when you have to turn them over. It's a little like working with a hibernating bear. Now the bear was awake.

"If you try to kill me, you're going to be in trouble!" Marion Huffnagle shouted at him.

"No Mrs. Huffnagle, I'm just trying to help get you dressed."

"You're trying to kill me and you're going to hear about it."

He remained quiet from that point on, silently helping her. All the while she continued to accuse him of plotting her demise. He finished with Mrs. Huffnagle and wheeled her to the dining room.

"Don't you leave me in here alone," she called out as he left. "I'll die in here."

Davis walked over to her to see if he could put her at ease.

"You get away from me," she shouted. "You're trying to kill me."

"Just go," the woman behind the kitchen counter said.

He walked to the next room. The occupant met him in the doorway.

"Good morning Delores," Davis said cheerily.

"I'll bet you're one of those jack-asses who wouldn't have sense enough to come in out of the rain," she growled and wheeled herself away from him.

"Best two out of three?" Davis said to himself then moved to the next room. The woman sitting inside was already dressed but in a loose-fitting, silk shirt. Davis knew that the second he got her into the dining room, she would complain about being cold.

"Mrs. Rogers would you like a sweater to put on? It's quite cool in the dining room."

She smiled and nodded politely. He smiled back and thought he at least made a basic connection with her. Davis threaded the sleeve of her sweater over her withered and clenched left arm.

"Ehhh, ttt. Ttttt. Eeeh!" she stuttered out in grand disapproval.

"I'm sorry Mrs. Rogers, I don't quite…"

"Ehhh!" she screamed. "Ttt rre Tttt!"

She swung at him with her good right arm and he nearly tripped over his feet backing out of the room. He walked quickly back toward the dining room and tried to remember why he agreed to come on this shift in the first place.

Oh, yeah. Certain death if I stayed on nights.

Davis took a deep breath and slowed his pace a little. He thought about Mrs. Rogers wheeling toward him, swinging her arm and how the sheer size and roundness of her glasses made her look like a very angry gray owl flapping its wing at him in half-blind rage.

"It's a little bit of what most of them go through every day."

Davis spun around to see who was speaking to him in these unfamiliar, calm and rational tones. It was one of the ladies from the kitchen.

"What did you say?" Davis asked.

"I said, it's a little bit of what they go through every day, what you're feeling right now. That mixture of frustration and exhaustion, rage and laughter at just how absurd life in this place really is."

Davis smiled in exhausted agreement.

"They don't like new faces. New faces mean change and they're not crazy about that either."

"I understand that."

"No you don't honey," she said. "For you, change means a new brand of underwear or maybe you have to cab it in here because you missed your bus. For them, change is a degrading road that leads them in here. On the surface this is a clean, friendly place for Momma and Daddy to spend the last of their magic golden years, but get just a little below the surface and you see it for what it really is, this is Death's warehouse. They are stacked up in here like cord wood until it is time for them to leave this life. Don't tell me you understand, you can't possibly. None of us can."

Davis lowered his head in humbled silence.

"I never thought of it like that," he said.

"It's okay, honey." She put a reassuring arm around him. "Nobody does."

She was a short, dark-skinned woman; likely no more than five feet tall and wore a uniform that barely contained her ample frame. The woman had a good heart, Davis could sense that the second they began to speak and there was a motherly tenderness about her, mixed with just enough good-natured playfulness to make him feel safe and warm the longer he was with her.

"Name of Violet Samson. I've been working in this place since the day it re-opened, I don't miss anything around this place, understand? Not anything. So if you want to know the truth of what happens around here, you just come ask me. If you want the truth, you just come ask Violet. We've all heard about you, they say you're the one."

"The what?" Davis sputtered.

He thought for a second that everyone knew about the things Jenn told him but was relieved to find out he wasn't the only one not in on a gigantic cosmic joke.

"The one male worker who is going to last more than a month here," said Violet.

Davis had been completely absorbed in listening to Violet that he forgot to bring residents down for breakfast when it dawned on him to turn around and get on with it. The last resident was being wheeled into the dining room by a very angry looking healthcare aid.

"If you could spare a moment." She glared at him and pushed a chair beside a white-haired woman who stared vacantly at the plate of food in front of her.

Davis sat down next to the woman and slid the chair in close to the table.

"Hi Anna, how about some breakfast?"

"Nope," said the white-haired woman who proceeded to hold her mouth open in anticipation of a spoonful of watery porridge.

Davis recognized Anna Klein as one of the few who were up during his rounds on the night shift. She prattled on endlessly in the dark, not making a great deal of sense but always having a great time.

"Anna, I'm going to change your brief." He would say to her every night.

"Beef, brief, beef thief of Baghdad and Dad's bag and you. Doo, doo, doo, doo, doo, la, la, la laaaahhhh." It would always end in singing which made

Davis' mood brighten whenever he left her room.

Now he sat beside her in the light of day, she was wide awake and twice as entertaining.

"Anna, don't you want anything to eat?" He put a spoonful into her open mouth.

"How should I know what they do with their motor goose feather?" Anna's words muffled around a mouthful of runny eggs.

The woman's stark white hair was cut too short by hairdressers who were more worried about lice than the appearance of their clients. Her skin, pale and thin, reminded Davis of slightly moist tissue paper—opaque and fragile looking, and if she moved just so, you could see her veins flex through it as she moved. But it was her eyes that left him speechless. He refused to turn on the room lights while he changed them at night and so in the dim illumination provided by the hallway, he hadn't really seen them. In the stark light of the dining room, he could scarcely see anything but them. They were ice blue, as magnificently blue as his own but for the pupil. The pupil was a tiny, infinitesimal black dot that threatened to disappear entirely if Anna should stare at something a little too long. It never moved, never got any larger or smaller no matter what the available light.

"Anna," he asked her again. "How about some red juice?"

She stuck out a hand and he took it tenderly.

"Where have you been hiding?" She took a gulp of juice.

He sat with her for a while after everyone left and continued to try and pour the red juice into her, despite objections. She managed to drink most of it and when he figured she was really finished, he pulled her away from the table and began to wheel her back to her room.

"Anna has square dancing in a couple of minutes," Violet called out. "Just leave her in the activities room."

"Ah you know she's in a wheelchair, right? Might make square dancing a little awkward."

"Stick around and help, you'll see," said Violet.

Davis wheeled Anna into the activities room, which was little more than a carpeted area to the right of the dining room. Soon, it filled with the residents from Davis' own floor, along with the residents from other floors brought by the activities and care staff from the other floors, all but three of whom were currently in wheelchairs.

"All right y'all, time to gather round!" called out one of the activities director exuberantly. She set a battered cd player on a dining table and pressed the play button and the old time square dance band began to plink and plunk away. The healthcare aides grabbed the wheelchairs, the three people who could walk stood up and the half speed dance macabre began. Davis pushed Anna in the circle, following the path of the wheelchair in front of him. It wasn't so much about dancing as it was walking in a circle and changing direction every time the woman from activities called out something square dancey. They all seemed to be enjoying it, even the ladies who were no longer capable of speech. The ones whose faces bore such grimaces of anguish. Expressions seemed to soften a little as they circled the room.

"Allemande left," the woman called out and they all walked in a circle going left.

"Promenade right." They all went right.

It went on like this for a time and the circle slowed to a stop. Davis became aware that Marion Huffnagle, Ida Rogers and Delores Smith were all staring intently at him.

Oh, no. They're getting ready to gang up on me.

The three women all stared at Davis with eyes narrowed as he wheeled Anna Klein round and round. Then without warning they stopped their own dancing and began to shout at him.

"Dance with me, Davis. Dance with me!"

"You old fool," said Delores. "He won't dance with you, you're a jackass."

"You're trying to kill me," said Marion Huffnagle. "Davis, she's trying to kill me."

"Ehf tttt, ttt. Ree ree Tttttt." said Ida Rogers.

Davis smiled and bent down to speak to Anna Klein, face to face.

"If you'll excuse me, Madame?" he asked her.

"I don't know," said Anna.

One by one he danced with them all, Marion and Delores and Ida. And one by one they all laughed and grew to love Davis in ways they hadn't only hours before, and just when he felt like he was really making a connection with them, his shift was over and it was time to leave.

"Are you in tomorrow?" Violet called out to him.

"As far as I know," answered Davis.

"Don't take it personally, but all three of them are going to forget you before tomorrow. You haven't put in your time, but feel good that they wanted you to dance with them on the first day. I've never seen them do that with anyone before. They like you, all three of them."

Davis beamed at her, as though she had just told him he'd won the lottery. In a way, he reasoned he had.

"I'll take what I can get," he laughed.

CHAPTER 16

Ezra Schneider walked up the steps of Winterbourne just past 10 PM. The older man was confident he could talk his way past the guard, though if being charming wasn't enough to make it past, the contents of the bag in his hand would assure a way in. He would keep quiet on one of the adjacent wards and, when the time was right, make his way down to Davis Mareth's ward and politely knock his ass out and throw him in a sack.

The night watchman sat at his desk, feet up, drinking a small cup of coffee and watched Family Feud. Ezra cleared his throat as he walked up to the desk.

"How can I help you?" asked the night watchman, never once taking his eyes off of the television.

"You can keep watching that bastarding squawk-box and make like you never saw me. Or I can take the lead pipe I brought out of this bag and I can brain you with it. Either way, I'm coming in here," Ezra said calmly.

"I didn't see nothing," said the night watchman.

Ezra strolled past him and headed toward a sturdy looking chain-link door.

"You can't get past the gate until I push the button," said the guard.

"Which you are pressing now, I expect?" Ezra asked.

The gate buzzed as the guard's finger depressed the button and Ezra Schneider walked through it into a blackened corridor. He closed his eyes and walked slowly forward, taking deep breaths as he did. The smell of this place hadn't changed any for all of the money they dumped into it. It still had the vague musty smell of a cottage near the water but the desperation that he knew existed in this place, made any thoughts of the warmth of a cottage disappear like a tear in the shower. He continued on, eyes still shut. The former orderly had worked in this place for so long that he had no problem walking in the darkened hallways; he knew every nook and cranny by heart.

Though the inky blackness around him made it nearly impossible to see, he sensed something shuffling past his feet and stopped suddenly. Ezra opened his eyes and examined the room. As his vision adjusted to the light, or lack of it, and he saw a clearer picture of his surroundings.

"Rats," he said to the empty room. "Place was always full of rats."

He walked toward the corridor's exit and he felt a definite something touch him as it moved past. This time, it brushed his knee and kept moving.

"Big bastarding rats!" he said.

The big bastarding rat stared at Ezra in the blackness through its black goggle eyes and tapped its long, razor sharp talons on the floor. It ran a black forked tongue over yellowed, needle teeth and shook dreadlocks behind its head. The creature hissed and squatted down on its hind legs, compressing them like a spring. The black eyed thing was ready to pounce when Ezra saw another like the first appear and hold a clawed hand.

"Sorry, Stevens, old boy. This is an unauthorized attack and completely against the rules, I'm afraid."

The second of the things was slightly larger and thicker and more sinewy muscled than the Stevens thing by at least half, and from the length and color of its dreadlocks, it appeared to be older.

"Oh, balls!" the Stevens thing griped.

"Sorry, can't be helped. You know how it goes. I let you attack the unsuspecting human and by Monday it's complete bloody chaos 'round the office," explained the older thing.

"I suppose you're right, Mr. MacAvoy," the Stevens thing said reluctantly.

It lowered its head in defeat and slunk away to a small dark spot in the room and then disappeared altogether. The MacAvoy thing let out a short howl and bared its lethal claws. Ezra had gotten quite a head start in the time it took to persuade Stevens to leave the human alone but he was not unreachable. MacAvoy breathed deep and prepared to sprint after him. Just as his first foot left the ground, a bell rang. Ezra stopped in his tracks and whipped his head around in the darkness trying to find the source of the sound.

"What the balls was that?"

The MacAvoy thing heard Ezra speak and wanted to call out to him, to tell him it was nothing to worry about, that it was just a warning bell, and then it wanted to tear his throat out and lap up his blood as he lay there listening to the final beats of his own heart. It sat back and smiled at the thought of the delicious terror-flavored meat of the human. A small yellow note feathered its way through the air in front of MacAvoy which read:

The human belongs to me. Not to be touched under any circumstances.

D.

The thing muttered its curses to Ezra Schneider and to the darkness, into which it promptly disappeared. Ezra Schneider considered that if, at 115 years-old, bells were the worst thing he was hearing than he was still doing pretty well and continued his search for Davis Mareth. He got to the door and managed to stay hidden in the shadows just as a figure walked past the double doors.

Ezra knew he wasn't to kill Davis, one of the small mercies afforded to him during all of this; still he had to get something away from him that he wasn't likely to give up without some kind of struggle. Rendering someone unconscious wasn't anything like killing and so he grabbed the lead pipe from his bag and headed for the nurse's station. He saw a linen closet that looked big enough to get him out of sight while still giving him enough light through the louvers to see Davis approach.

The old man settled into the closet and put his hand in his pocket. The picture was there, it was always there. He wondered what his daughter would make of the man he had become. All the things he promised her, all the words he had ever said, to help her to be a fulfilled and wholesome person, gone up like so much meaningless smoke. He was certain that she died hating his memory, he deserved no better and that was far worse a punishment than anything he had experienced thus far. Ezra could live to be a thousand and never forgive himself for the shame he brought on his child. He flicked the corner of the picture in his pocket and felt the bite of tears prick at his eyes.

"Why daddy?" he heard the little blonde girl say.

"Oh please, baby, not now," Ezra called out to the empty closet.

"Why Daddy, why did you hurt that lady."

"Oh baby, I'm so sorry," Ezra began to cry out loud, alone in the dark closet. "I just wanted things to be better for us… for you. If I could take it back I would, baby. I'd be stronger, I would have come home to you instead of going to that room. I know you don't believe it, but Daddy is not a bad man. I am not a bad man."

He sat in the closet sobbing and quickly came to the decision that he had had just about enough of all of this trying to cheat death nonsense because the only one really cheating death was him and everyone around him, all the people he loved, were still very much dead. That was it then, he was finished with Nancy Seasons and all of her spooky horseshit.

"Fuck this balls up bullshit," Ezra said. "I'm going home."

He stood up and opened the closet door, fully expecting to have to come up with some kind of logical explanation as to why he was in this closet so late at night. Hell, he could even ask this Mareth if he would just give him the goddamned book, it was worth a shot right?

Ezra stepped out of the closet and saw the figure asleep at the desk. Beside the figure, was a black and white composition book that Ezra could likely grab without alerting the sleeping figure but just the same, he took the lead pipe out of his bag and held it above the sleeper's head. He noiselessly grabbed the book and the figure's head shot up like a rocket.

"Hey!" said a startled Ezra. "Hey, you're not a goddamned guy."

"What are you doing out of bed?" the young woman said. "And that's my goddamned book."

Ezra looked at the book, which was now firmly in the grasp of the surprised young nursing student and looked at the lead pipe in his hand. He didn't have to think too hard before the lead pipe made its way to the woman's head and the book was in his hand. Tucking it and the lead pipe into his bag, he headed for the double doors. The old man stopped before he left the ward and looked back to the nurse's station.

"I know, I know," he said and walked back into the nurse's station. He picked the slender young woman up and laid her gingerly on the worn chesterfield in the meeting room. After walking into the kitchen and filling a large plastic bag with ice, he went back to the woman and placed the bag under her head.

Ezra looked around the room for a first aid kit and took the smelling salts from it. He put the vial under the woman's nose and twisted it until it broke open and waited until she started to come around then headed out the double doors. Nancy was very specific about the book, the black and white composition book. Maybe this Davis Mareth she told him about had lent it to one of his co-workers. At any rate, she would get her damned book and what's more, nobody wound up with anything worse than a bad headache in the getting of it. Ezra Schneider was certain he could go home now and get ready to die.

CHAPTER 17

"Jimmy," Lois called out to him. "Jimmy, come here." The elderly woman looked around as though somebody might be following her. She ushered Davis into her room and quickly shut the door.

"If I tell you something," Lois began ominously, "promise me that you won't think I've gone off my head."

"Okay, Lois," Davis said earnestly. "What is it?"

"You remember I told you about the man in my closet, right?"

Davis wondered how it would sound if a person, who was already nutty, went off their head?

"I remember you told me something about him," he said warily.

"Last night," she began to whisper. "I saw the lights come on in my closet and I thought he might be coming for a visit. He still does from time to time, you know. So I sat in my armchair over there and waited for him to come out…" She walked over to the chair and sat down.

Davis saw a look of solid fear crawl across her face and worried she descended into a type of hallucination that she might not come back from.

"Lois, what happened? Who came in this room last night?"

Davis began to panic and mentally rushed to places he shouldn't go. He knew that there were people capable of depravity so unimaginable that he could scarcely get his head around it but in his heart, he didn't feel this was where she was going. In his short time at Winterbourne, Davis had learned that losing your mind was far from the worst thing that could happen to you here.

"Lois, tell me what happened."

She sat in her chair and stared out the window at a blue sky full of clouds she would never get any closer to than this. A gentle breeze she would never feel blew the treetops. She closed her eyes and she could almost smell the cedar. The look of fear vanished and was replaced by a look of contentment.

"I never married, Jimmy," Lois began.

"Lois… " Davis stammered. "I don't-"

"I never married because I didn't want to be tied down. Not to anybody or anything. I traveled many places and I knew a lot of men, but I never grew roots anywhere and now I am a foolish old woman who is spending the last days of her life locked in this pensioner's prison."

"Marriage isn't all it's cracked up to be," Davis said, trying to sound helpful, though he truthfully had no idea what exactly marriage was cracked up to be.

"No that's not what I mean, I don't regret anything. When he first came out of my closet, my friend, I thought I was losing my mind, but we had such chemistry that I just knew he had to be real. As impossible as I knew it was, I knew somewhere, deep down, that it wasn't a lonely, addled old brain playing tricks. It was always the same, the lights in the closet would come on and out he'd come. We spent days and days together, Jimmy."

She paused and smiled and Davis took her hand.

"I fell in love with him and I fell hard, so when he told me he had to leave I didn't understand why. Had I done something? One day he just stopped coming by and I haven't seen him since. So when the lights came on in the closet last night, I was so excited I could barely stand it. But it wasn't my friend that came out of that closet."

"What was it?" Davis beamed, completely enthralled with what she said.

"They were small, about the size of children," Lois said. "But they weren't children at all. They were terrible looking things, all raggedy hair and claws and teeth."

Davis felt a knot form in the pit of his stomach. She was describing the terrible, brutish things he had seen and suddenly this all became very real.

"There were two or three of them and they started circling around me, clawing at the ground and grunting and sniffing around me like they were a pack of ravenous wolves. They took turns swatting at my face, I put my arms up and they scratched at them until I put them back down. I thought they would have a go at my face then but they just kept circling me and grunting and sniffing."

Davis couldn't believe what he was hearing; this woman had met up with the vicious porcupine Rastafarian things and lived to tell about it.

"Were you scared?" Davis asked.

"You're kidding me, right? Three gruesome children were circling me and moving in for the kill? I wished I had a diaper because I near crapped my pants."

He began to speak and she cut him off.

"Just when I thought they were going to finish me off, I heard a voice from the closet."

"Was it him? Was it your friend from the closet?" Davis asked.

"No," she said. "And yes. It was a voice that was so familiar, like his and yet so strange. It was soft and full of comfort but just the same I was aware of a terrible power behind that voice. Like my mother's voice wrapped in a clap of thunder."

"What did it say?" Davis asked excitedly.

Here was someone who had experienced all of the terrible things he had seen since coming to this place and she was still able to talk about it.

"It wasn't what it said so much," Lois replied. "It was the way it said it. All it said was, 'NO.' But the voice was so quiet, so soft I could barely hear it and so mighty the walls were shaking. The three things around me froze and ran and hid when they saw him come out of my closet."

"So it was him, your friend." Davis said, feeling as though he had come to a great realization.

"No," Lois said. "It was a boy. A beautiful, pale-skinned, little boy with the most delicate black wings I have ever seen. There was a light coming off of him that those three things couldn't bear the sight of and ran away from as quickly as they had come into my room. His cheeks were so red—apple-cheeked my mother always called it—he looked like he had just come in from ice skating and was waiting for a cup of hot cocoa to warm him up. And his eyes, oh his eyes were bluer than any kind of blue I ever seen. They were... they were a lot like your eyes, Jimmy."

"I've seen him, Lois. I've seen that little boy. The night old Arthur Grant passed. He came out of Arthur's closet and kissed him on the forehead," Davis said.

"He kissed my head too," Lois said. "He kissed my head and then he whispered in my ear and walked back into the closet."

Davis was suddenly very confused. The night the little boy emerged from Arthur Grant's closet was the night Arthur Grant passed on. He was certain that night that he knew who the little boy was. But Lois Helm sat there still very much among the living. It was the how and the why that Davis couldn't make sense of.

"Lois," Davis began. "What did the little boy whisper in your ear?"

"He said not to tell anyone until the time was right and I would know when that was and as soon as I saw you tonight, I knew that time was now. What do you suppose it all means Jimmy?"

Davis looked at her and felt the tears well up in his eyes. He kissed her forehead.

"I don't know Lois, I don't know," he lied.

Davis hugged his friend and didn't want to let her go. He didn't know why she managed to remain alive after her visit from the winged boy while Arthur Grant had passed, but what he knew for certain that her already ticking clock was now in a flat out run and his heart was breaking for her.

CHAPTER 18

"**D**isappointed!" Nancy Seasons yelled from the seat behind her oversized desk.

"Excuse me?" asked Ezra Schneider.

"Apparently there is no excuse for you, yes?" Nancy said in the insipid tone she reserved strictly for people she felt were beneath her. "Brought the wrong book, yes? And taken from the wrong person, yes?"

"You can spare me the angry school marm voice. It doesn't frighten me and makes you sound like a pinhead, yes?" Ezra said, mockingly. "Look it, you said you wanted a black and white composition book from the person working the nightshift. That is what you got."

"I told you to get a black and white composition book from the MALE person working the night shift. A black and white composition book, in fact, that contained the only ritual capable of summoning and trapping Death."

Ezra looked at Nancy blankly.

"Was it a male you got this book from?"

"No," said Ezra. "It was a cute little skinny girl with bad teeth."

"Ah," said Nancy. "A cute little skinny girl with bad teeth, indeed. Did you happen to examine the contents of the black and white composition book she had with her, the one you did take?"

The older man glowered at Nancy as she pushed the book into his face.

"No," Ezra growled. His ire was beginning to rise. He didn't like all of this smoke and mirrors mumbo jumbo to begin with, he had heard it before and from people he respected a lot more than Nancy-goddamned-Seasons. The old man was tired of it all and he didn't remotely want to entertain the prospect of having to do more things that would push him further and further away from anything that still resembled humanity. He absolutely could not bear that this halfwit woman felt she was his better because she had figured a way to hold him hostage within his own guilt. Ezra reached out a hand to take the book from her. Nancy jerked the book back before the old man could get his hands on it.

"If you had bothered to have a look at the book, you would have seen it was the wrong one. The book that Mareth has is full of diagrams and incantations. Does that look like an incantation to you?"

She opened the first page of the book and held it in front of his face. Ezra tried not to smile as Nancy raged in front of him. He didn't try very hard.

"What does it say Ezra?"

He remained silent, biting his lip.

"You will wipe that stupid grin off of your face and read the first page, yes?"

The smile fell off his lips and the anger burned up the back of his neck, he looked down at the black and white composition book.

"I love Adam Harper," he said through clenched teeth.

"Whoa," spat Nancy. "Is that Death creeping up behind you? You know, for years I thought that Death's true identity was Hades, the lord of the underworld."

Nancy Seasons begun to unravel entirely. She raved and Ezra could detect, although very slight, the trace of a southern accent that many years of elocution lessons in some overpriced New England private school had tried to erase.

"But no," she continued. "It turns out the Master of the Void's real name is Adam Fucking Harper!"

"Now look," Ezra interrupted.

She was far beyond being reasoned with at this point.

"No, you look, you forsaken, fucking relic. I don't care what you do but you get that book. I don't give a good goddamn if you have to run over that kid's head with a school bus, just get me that book. Preferably the book that actually has some witchy looking bits in it and not pink fucking hearts!"

She threw the false book at Ezra and he caught it in midair. He stood burning with rage and took a deep breath, carefully contemplating what he would say next.

"I will go get you this other book and I will help you perform your goddamn ceremony and I will even kill this man of yours if I need to, but once I have done this, you will keep your promise to me. Because if you don't, I will bury the spine of that bastarding book deep into your skull and I will stand over you and look into your shit brown eyes and I will be the last thing you ever see in this life."

Ezra could see from the look in her eyes that Nancy appreciated the gravity of what he was saying.

Nancy however, didn't flinch.

"See that you do," she said barely louder than a whisper. "Someone has altered my files and put him on the day shift. You can't very well just walk onto a ward full of geriatrics and do away with him; you'll have to do it after he finishes work."

"I'll figure it out," Ezra said.

Nancy turned to leave, but turned back.

"There is a very small window of opportunity to perform this ritual and for me to give you what you want. We have two days before the next rise of the full moon. After the moon begins to wane, we are out of luck for another thousand years. Even if Death hasn't named a successor."

"Cripes," Ezra grumbled. "More magical crap."

Ezra walked out into the morning air and headed for his car. He turned the key back and forth several times and when the loud whirring noise of the engine trying to catch refused to turn into the purring of a well-oiled machine, he got out and kicked the door shut.

"Isn't that just grand," he said. "Even if I don't have to kill this fucking guy, I'm going to kill this fucking guy.

He zipped up his coat and began the three-mile trek up hill to Winterbourne.

CHAPTER 19

Davis Mareth lay in his bed awake, turning what Lois had told him over and over in his mind and thinking of the little winged boy he saw in Arthur Grant's room the night of his death. He felt certain it was the small boy he had seen on one of the glass doors in his dream, though it seemed less like it was a dream and more like his body went for a walk and only casually mentioned it to his mind. Davis couldn't be sure how he knew it, but this beautiful boy was Death, he felt it in his bones.

Maybe his skeleton suit was at the cleaners?

He also knew this same little boy visited Lois Helm and no matter how many different ways he looked at it, he couldn't think of a single way to save his friend's life.

"But I can!" He sat bolt upright in bed and shouted to the empty room, "I am Death's successor. Jenn said I was his heir. I can take the robe and the scythe and then Lois doesn't have to go anywhere."

Davis dressed quickly and stuffed the black and white composition book into his backpack followed by a very unimaginative lunch. He had to see Jenn but wasn't sure how. Wasn't she a ghost type thing? She should be able to read his thoughts and just appear at will, right? He half expected her to be standing behind him and when she wasn't, he grabbed his backpack and ran for the bus.

Nancy Seasons lay in her bed, awake, turning her meeting with Ezra Schneider and the letter from the director over and over in her mind. Her time was running out and her faith in Ezra finding the book in time faded quicker than the beating heart of the old woman tied to the armchair beside her bed. She wanted to believe everything would go smoothly and Ezra would deliver the book just as she slit Davis' throat. That he would die and she would assume the mantle of death and wield a power as beautiful and terrible as the wretchedness in her own heart. But she knew it wasn't going to happen.

"Unless," she said and sat bolt upright in bed. "I can get the book myself and cut that Schneider fool out completely, yes?"

"I could kill the Mareth Boy myself and then read the ritual and when Death arrives, he will submit to my will and then the world will really change, yes?"

She dressed quickly and stuffed a black messenger bag with things she thought she needed; the black velvet robes the director left her, the ones with strange markings on either arm and the 'Melvin's Boxeteria' logo on the back, a small truncheon to subdue Davis when she met up with him and a very unimaginative lunch. Nancy had to find Davis and she knew, almost to the room number, where he would be this morning. To her own amusement, she half expected Death to be standing right in front of her, trying to prevent her from succeeding in what she was about to undertake. When Death didn't show, she grabbed the bag and ran for her car.

Davis ran up the steps to Winterbourne Home just as the rain began and hurried down to the locker room. He changed quickly and headed up to the ward. Jenn must have tuned in on his thoughts by now, he supposed. He started his shift with no sign of her and began to wonder if Jenn Henderson and he were on the same page at all. She had said that one of the benefits of being dead was the ability to read his mind, yet there was no sign of her.

"Jimmy," Lois called to him from her door way. "It's him, he's here right now."

It didn't register with Davis right away. He was too excited that he had a way to save her.

"Lois, it's okay," he gushed. "I figured it out and everything is going to be okay now."

"What's going to be okay?" Lois asked. "Didn't you hear what I said? I said he's here, right now. HE'S here right now. My friend is."

"Wait, what?" Davis asked. "He's in your room right now?"

"Yes," Lois said. "Come on and I'll show you."

He forgot about Jenn for the moment and went to Lois' room to meet the man from the closet. If there were any pangs of scepticism left in him about Lois's friend from the closet, they were cemented when he walked through her door. The room was empty.

"I don't understand, Jimmy," Lois said quietly.

Davis felt her disappointment and his own. He knew she hadn't imagined the boy with the black wings or the dreadlocked things that came before—he saw those things himself, but the man living in the closet was something altogether different. It dawned on him that from the first time she mentioned the man that it might have been the longings of a mind that was growing more clouded as she got older and it seemed now, that's exactly what it was.

"It's all right Lois; there will be plenty of other times to meet him."

A knowing smile came to him and he hugged her.

"He was here Jimmy, he was. Wasn't he?" Her voice trailed off and she sat down in her worn, faded arm chair and stared silently out the window for a time.

"Am I losing my mind, Jimmy?" Lois finally said, breaking the silence.

She suddenly seemed very small and frail to him. Gone was the brazen and stubborn woman who scared the life out of him his first shift, who he felt didn't really belong in this place. In her place was an ashen, faded old woman who was all at once frightened by a cruel and unrelenting world that was threatening to collapse in on her.

"I can't live like this," Lois whispered.

"I know, Lois," said Davis.

He folded a blanket across her lap and took her hand. In an instant he got a flash of the woman she had been. She was full of life and beautiful and running to the bus station carrying an empty Gladstone bag. Her mother shouted she would need clothes, a toothbrush, something… anything, but the young girl said she would get new clothes and things in the city. It was a fresh start. Davis could see that only a few months later, that beautiful girl was sitting alone in a small, poorly lit room. She sported a black eye and stared at the telephone, wanting desperately to pick it up and tell her mother how scared and lonely she was here but refused to let herself be weak. Later still, he saw a middle-aged woman sitting alone on a cold iron bench in a park, watching young mothers walk by with their children. Wishing sometimes that her life had taken a different path and in what Davis felt no more than a heartbeat, that woman was walking up the steps of Winterbourne and trying desperately to put a stopper on the life she had fought so hard to free all those years ago.

Lois drifted off to sleep. Davis pulled the blanket up around her shoulders and began to walk out.

He looked back to her, wanted to say something noble and profound to her. Even though she couldn't hear him, he wanted her to know he would make things better for her, that she didn't need to feel afraid of the world outside or inside of Winterbourne anymore. He would make it all right… for her.

Davis walked out of her room more determined than ever not to let her die. He walked past the nurse's station and caught something out of the corner of his eye. If it was one of those things, he thought they were out early. He looked to the double doors and into the darkened hallway of one of the empty wings and saw Jenn Henderson standing there, motioning for him to come to her. Davis practically ran to her.

"I need to meet him, Jenn," Davis said stoically.

"Meet who?" she asked.

"Your boss, you know, the skeleton guy."

"He wants to meet you too but not yet."

"What?" Davis asked incredulous. "What do you mean, not yet? Shouldn't I meet the guy I'm going to take over for?"

"You can't do it, Davis."

"What?" Davis asked.

"You can't do what you are planning to do. I'm sorry but you just can't."

"But I'll be Death, right?" he asked indignantly, "The Servant of the Void. I can decide who lives and who dies."

"I'm sorry Davis," she said.

"I want to meet this guy right now!" he demanded, and began to walk out of the darkened hallway, angry and confused.

"Davis, wait!" Jenn begged.

He made it to the double doors and stopped. His head lowered and he sobbed. He wept and reached out for the mother he had never really known and he wept for Lois and just how unfair life and death really were. In his heart he knew that Jenn was right and he couldn't save his friend and it was tearing him up inside.

Davis turned back toward the darkened hallway and found, to his surprise, that she had crossed the hallway in an instant and now stood next to him. She took his head tenderly in her hands and kissed him. He found himself resisting her embrace but his heart took him where his mind was not willing to let him go. For the moment he forgot about Death and Lois Helm and Winterbourne Home and how profoundly sad all of this was and kissed her back.

She pulled away from him just long enough to smile and take his hand.

"Come on," she said.

Jenn led Davis down the hallway and into a large, darkened room. The room became bathed in the glow of the candles she lit. There were pieces of furniture covered by moving blankets and large pieces of canvas.

"This is going to be Nancy's new office, yes?"

Davis laughed.

"The work won't be done in here for at least a month."

She pulled the moving blanket off a comfortable looking, overstuffed couch and pushed him down onto it. Jenn kissed him and there was an urgency in it that made Davis' heart pound. Eagerly and without a word, she climbed on top of him and removed her uniform top, took his hand and placed it on her breast. Her skin was warm, which he thought a little strange, but he imagined if she was not he might not have been such a willing participant. He leaned into her and kissed her breast. She pushed her chest closer into his face as she reached around behind him to remove his own shirt.

The dark haired woman made little kisses on the side of his neck which turned to little nips of her teeth and little flicks of the end of her tongue. She moved slowly down to his chest and Davis could feel his breath start to quicken watching her as she tried to match the rhythm of his breathing, every time his chest would rise, the tip of her tongue would flick out to meet it.

Davis leaned in and began to caress the back of her neck and let his tongue gingerly explore the small area just behind her earlobe. She let out a soft and low moan and he cupped her breasts in his hands. He ran his fingers softly over them, traveling every delicate curve of her. His hand went around to her back and he dragged his fingertips down, softly at first and then pushing them hard enough that if he had used his fingernails, he would have made her bleed. Jenn moaned again and arched her back as he dragged his fingers down again.

She peered up from his chest with a look that Davis never saw her make before. Her eyes held a mischievous gaze and she ran her tongue over her teeth. She leaned down and bit his neck.

"Ow," he said with a laugh.

It hurt, but not enough to dissuade him from letting her continue, which she happily did. Davis continued to drag his hands down her back until she reached around and grabbed them. Her grip was surprisingly strong and Davis felt that, even if he really wanted to, he might not be able to get away from her. Not that he really wanted to. She took his hand, never taking her mouth off of his neck and guided it to the front of her uniform pants. With her other hand she untied the pants drawstring. She looked up and stared into his eyes with a look that made him ache for her. She slipped his hand inside her pants.

He flattened the palm of his hand against her and cupped his fingers toward the back of her. She was warm and he could feel the moisture and the soft hair against his palm. He moved his hand slowly back and then forward again and she convulsed a little and let out a shuddering breath. Davis moved his hand back and forth again and she raised her hips in time with his hand. He gave her a look and she mouthed the word 'yes'. Moving his hand back again, she shifted her hips slightly back to accommodate him and he gently introduced a finger inside of her. She bit down hard against his neck.

Jenn moaned with the motions of his hand and pushed her hips back and forth to match the movement of his fingers. She ran her fingers through his hair and tugged and pulled at it as she began to take gulps of air. Grabbing his hand and raising it up, she rubbed it against her face and swirled her tongue around his fingers one by one. The woman got off his lap and stood in front of him, as she did, her untied pants hit the floor and Davis could see she wasn't wearing underwear.

Davis leaned up slightly and pulled her close to him, so that his face met her navel. He turned his face into her and slowly and repeatedly kissed her belly with a passion he didn't know he had in himself. Pushing her back a little, he looked up at her naked form. She was glorious. He rose up to face her and found himself not wanting to leave her gaze.

Jenn couldn't take any more; she pulled him up to her and pushed her mouth on to Davis', her wanting tongue forced its way past his lips and began a familiar dance. Her hands groped and found the waist band of his pants. She thrust them down and when they became caught around his knees, her foot came up and pushed them the rest of the way down. Forcefully shoved him back down onto the overstuffed couch and crawled upon his lap.

He felt her skin against his and put his hands on her bottom pulling her closer and without much effort, he was in her. She pulled at his hair and he was inflamed with every tug of her fingers.

Davis pushed up with his hips as she pushed down with hers and she pulled harder at his hair. He pushed harder and she pulled harder. They began moving as one. She stopped pulling his hair and held his face again.

Jenn stared into his eyes, his beautiful impossibly blue eyes. She pulled his face closer and kissed him with a warmth and comfort that wrapped around him like an old pair of jeans.

"Thank you," she whispered into his ear. The dark haired woman sat fully upright on his lap so that when she embraced him her breasts were in his face. He kissed her breasts briefly and then pulled her into him tightly as he could without hurting her. Davis felt complete, he felt pure and innocent. She looked radiant and beautiful. They felt loved.

CHAPTER 20

"Oh shit," said the charge nurse as she spat coffee all over her computer screen.

She just caught sight of Nancy Seasons walking her way and knew it never amounted to anything good when she came onto the ward.

"I am looking for Davis Mareth," Nancy stated.

The nurse stared blankly back at her.

"Davis Mareth, the man from the night shift. The only man who works in this entire goddamned nursing home, yes?"

The nurse knew who she was talking about and she had seen Davis walk off the ward more than an hour ago. It was a slow day, there weren't any issues with any of the residents and the charge nurse quite liked Davis and didn't want to see him get into any trouble.

"I know who he is, Nancy," the nurse said. "And I think he is bathing Mrs. Davison."

The nurse knew Nancy Seasons had limits she was not willing to go beyond and barging in on a resident during something as private as a bath was a place even she wouldn't go. Although she bet if she told Nancy that Davis was helping somebody put their shoes on, she still wouldn't have gone anywhere near the room. Nancy Seasons, for all the awards and certificates in her office, gave off the distinct impression that the elderly made her skin crawl.

The director faced down the charge nurse and felt the anger rise up in her.

"I am looking for something he is carrying, does he have a briefcase or a bag of some kind?" she asked.

"I don't know," the charge nurse replied. "And if I did, I certainly wouldn't condone you rifling through it. You'll just have to wait until he comes back here and you can ask him about it yourself."

"Very well," Nancy said. "I'll just sit here and wait for him."

She sat down in one of the uncomfortable arm chairs strewn around the nurse's meeting room. The young nurse looked at her watch and began to count.

Nancy Seasons heaved a sigh and stood up.

"Tell Mr. Mareth to come and see me in my office when he gets back here, please."

She walked out of the Nurse's station and walked down the corridor toward her office. When she was completely out of sight and earshot, the young charge nurse said, "Two and a half minutes, Nancy. That's a new record."

Nancy Seasons clomped back to her office with visions of all of the terrible things she was going to do to Davis Mareth dancing through her head. She would teach him what it was to suffer before the end. Maybe she would let him drown in his own blood rather than killing him outright. She smiled at the thought of him frothing at the mouth, choking and sputtering big crimson bubbles. Walking by the darkened hallway that led to her new office, Nancy thought she might head down it and into her office while her mind continued to dwell on Mareth and all the things she could do to him. When she thought she heard something as she walked by and stopped to look through the windows of the double doors, she pushed one of the doors open and stuck her head through it. Nancy couldn't be certain but it seemed to her to be hushed voices and low moans she was hearing. She stepped full into the blackened hallway now and stood for a moment as her eyes adjusted to the dark and listened hard in the blackness.

It was a man's voice, unmistakably, coming from her new office and a woman's too, but there was something else, something ephemeral. A kind of scratching like rats skimming along shards of broken earthenware and the sound was moving, closer to her office and closer to her. She froze but not out of fear. Rather, she didn't know what to do next. Investigate the scratching sound or find out who currently occupied her new office. She began to move toward her new office, reasoning that at least she would be within a confined area with a door and could shut out whatever was making the scratching noise, providing she made it there quickly enough. She could deal with whoever was responsible for the voices when she got there. It was likely nothing more than an orderly and a care worker, Nancy thought, fondling and groping each other in the darkness and it would be the highlight to an otherwise lackluster day as she handed each their walking papers.

As Nancy Seasons turned a determined foot toward her new office and the voices coming from it, she heard the desk phone ring from her present, cramped office.

"Goddamn it." She turned back toward the double doors and hurried to answer the phone.

The director got to her office too late to answer the phone, but no matter, time was running out on her and she couldn't spare even a second on anyone else's petty problems.

Nancy paced in the small space available behind her large oak desk. She could keep going back up to the ward, waiting for Mareth to be available and then just ask him for the book.

"Or," she said to the empty room, "I could wait for him to leave and just take it from him."

Nancy wasn't anywhere nearly as strong or powerful as her size suggested, but she was clever and, what's more, she had a truncheon in her bag. She decided to wait in the thicket at the bottom of the stairs and as Mareth passed by on his way home, she would bash him, take the book and get him into the room where she was going to perform the transference of power ritual, somehow. Doubting that she would be strong enough to move him on her own once he had been rendered him unconscious, the director decided she would need one of the custodians to wait with her. The two of them would subdue Davis easily, after she bashed him, and then move him together to whatever room was suitable to use for the ritual. Nancy smiled. Soon, she thought. The end game would begin, Davis would die and she would become the true servant of the eternal blackness of the void.

Ezra Schneider stood in the glass-walled bus shelter and looked at his watch. Nancy Seasons told him that the Mareth kid would be leaving Winterbourne shortly after two and it was nearly one-thirty now. There was enough time to hide himself in the bushes at the foot of the stairs and spring himself on the unsuspecting man as he walked by. He wouldn't be overly violent with him if he didn't need to be, but he would get that goddamned book away from Mareth one way or the other and then, maybe he would cram the book up Nancy Seasons' ass on principle.

"Relic, huh?" Ezra muttered.

"Pardon?" asked the twenty-something girl waiting for her bus.

"I said mind your business, ass-balls," Ezra replied and stomped out of the bus shelter.

It wasn't raining as much as a heavy mist was falling but it was enough moisture in the air that more than a few minutes in, it would begin to soak through your clothes and chill you to the bone. Not unlike squatting behind some bushes for 30 minutes or so in it would do.

"Sitting on my ass in the dirt, in the bastarding rain, waiting for some snot-nosed, little urchin to come waltzing out of this place so I can ask him for a goddamned book?" Ezra said to himself. "I am 115, I am too old for this kind of twaddle. You'll do as you're told or I'll make you suffer, yes?" He put his hands into his pockets to warm them and felt the picture. The old man breathed a heavy sigh and looked skyward.

"At least it's not pouring," Ezra said in the second it took before sky opened up.

 CHAPTER 21

"How does it feel to be a necrophiliac?" Jenn asked.

Davis hadn't really thought of it like that until just now and, though he just slept with a woman who had been dead longer than he'd been alive, he felt surprisingly good about it.

"Very alive," he replied, "and a little hungry."

Jenn hugged Davis' head and brought it into her chest. She kissed the top of his head and stood.

"I've got to go and you need to get back on the floor," She said.

"I know," he agreed. "I've been away long enough. I need to go back and check on…"

"You can't do it Davis," she said candidly. "I know what you're thinking and you're not the first one who ever thought of it. It doesn't work that way. I can't explain it to you but the boss will when you see him."

Davis sighed and finished dressing.

"I know," he said dejectedly. "I think I always knew; I just didn't want to believe it."

Jenn took Davis' hand.

"I'm sorry," she said. "I wish it could be different."

She kissed him passionately and held him longer than she thought she should have but when he didn't break away from the embrace, she didn't let him go.

"Okay," she kissed him again. "See you later?"

Davis released her hand and reached for his shirt.

"Of course," he replied.

There was a profound sadness in his voice that hadn't been there before. He stood and watched her walk away, wanting to call out something to her that might make her come back and say something to lessen the load he was carrying on his shoulders. When nothing better than it'll be OK came to him, she headed toward the wall at the back of the room. Davis watched her wave at the wall and a section of it opened inward to reveal a set of stone stairs. She began to climb the stairs and the moving wall closed outward behind her.

Davis Mareth entered the nurse's station and was greeted by the young charge nurse.

"I don't think I want to know where you were," she began.

"I don't think you'd believe me if I told you," Davis blushed.

"No, I likely wouldn't," the nurse said. "Nancy Seasons was poking around down here looking for you. She wanted to look through your bag."

"Did she?" Davis asked sounding a little agitated. "Look through my bag, I mean."

"No," said the nurse. "I lied and told her I didn't know which was yours."

Davis grabbed his backpack from under the desk and looked inside. Everything was as he had left it, right down to the uninteresting lunch that would now be an uninteresting dinner.

"Thanks, Carol," he said.

"Don't mention it," she said. "Next time you leave the floor, you have to let somebody other than me know, deal?"

"Deal," Davis said and headed for the exit.

"Oh, hey," the nurse called out. "Lois Helm had a fall; I know you are pretty fond of her. Maybe you should go see her before you leave; I have a feeling she isn't going to hold out for long. She was unconscious when we found her and she is nearly unresponsive now."

Davis dropped his backpack and ran to Lois' room. She lay on the bed, blankets pulled up to her throat and, were it not for the sound of her breathing, he'd have though she was already gone.

"Oh Lois, no," he said to the sleeping woman.

Her face was nearly as white as the sheets that covered her body and her eyes were partially closed. It looked as though she was trying to shut them and ran out of steam somewhere just before the top lid met up with the bottom. Her breathing was rough and uneven, but it was steady and Davis took a little hope from that.

"I wasn't here," he said remorsefully. "If I'd have been here, you wouldn't have fallen and—awe, fuck!"

Davis sat on the bed beside her and wept. His friend lay dying and he was powerless to help her.

"Lois, I know you can still hear me," he said through the tears.

"You promise me that you won't go anywhere."

He took her hand in his and kissed it gently.

"Not until tomorrow night okay, Lois?"

To his surprise, she squeezed his hand. She was still in there somewhere and she had heard what he said. He kissed the old woman's forehead and got up from the bed.

"I'll see you tomorrow," he said to her then headed to the nurse's station. Davis grabbed his backpack off the floor where he'd left it and headed out the door. He turned up the collar of his jacket out of habit but stood at the top of the stairs and looked skyward, letting the pouring rain soak him anyway. The young man walked slowly down the steps as the tears and cold stinging rain mixed freely on his face.

CHAPTER 22

E zra Schneider glanced at his watch. Two-thirty. He'd be damned if he could figure out how this kid managed to sneak past him without as much as a sound. The older man hadn't fallen asleep, though he certainly wanted to. He hadn't even closed his eyes more than two or three times since he sat down nearly an hour ago. Ezra had remained on this spot, gaze fixed on the top of the concrete staircase.

"Balls on all of this sitting wet-assed in the dirt horseshit." He stood and looked to the top of the stairs where Davis Mareth was now standing.

"All right, no more cloak and dagger soft soap," he said and started walking toward the staircase. The old man put his hand inside the leather bag and gripped the lead pipe tightly.

Nancy Seasons and her orderly squatted in the bushes at the foot of the stairs for about 25 minutes and Nancy already had enough of it 15 minutes ago.

"I don't know how, but that young man seems to have gotten by you, yes?" Nancy said with poisonous sweetness.

The custodian gritted his teeth and nodded to her.

"Yes Ma'am," he forced.

"I am running out of time," she snarled, all of her sweetness disappeared with every word spat at him. "Do you understand that? I have to get something vitally important from this man and get him all sorted out before midnight tomorrow and I can't very well do that if he isn't fucking here, yes?"

She stood and faced away from the stairs, readying herself to leave. The orderly stood beside her and pointed toward the staircase.

"Nancy, look!" he exclaimed.

She was about to scream at him for daring to call her Nancy when she saw what he pointed at.

Davis Mareth stood at the top of the staircase beginning his descent and Ezra Schneider was halfway up the staircase, rushing to meet Davis.

"What is that old fool doing?" she asked the custodian.

She squatted back down and pulled the orderly beside her.

Nancy thought about it and the old fool was doing exactly as she wanted him to do. Even though things weren't going as she had imagined, her getting the book from Ezra and the end result would be the same regardless. Still, she was a little disappointed at losing the chance to bash Mareth on the head and lead him away to the basement.

"We'll wait until they've gone," said Nancy.

"Yes Ma'am."

Nancy watched as Ezra and Davis walked calmly down the stairs and disappeared around the corner. She thought the grizzled old bugger was pretty clever for not thumping Mareth out in the open when she noticed the nurse from Davis' ward walking down the stairs. The nurse neared the bushes where Nancy and the orderly squatted. Nancy pounced.

"Any port in a storm." Nancy bashed the poor girl's skull from behind with the thick black truncheon. She took the red cable ties out of her pocket and passed them to the custodian. "Take her downstairs and tie her up."

"Yes Ma'am!" he crowed.

Ezra Schneider jogged up the stairs toward the man standing atop of them. He looked up to the heavens then glanced down for a second to notice the gray haired man running toward him, only to look back up again immediately after.

"Are you Mareth?" Ezra asked him.

There was no reply from him except the odd sniffle coming from a rain soaked face.

"Hey!" Ezra commanded. "Are you Davis Mareth?"

"Yeah," Davis said without looking down, "I am."

Ezra walked the last three steps and stood facing Davis, whose face was still pointed upward. He was easily a whole head taller than the younger man, so Ezra could practically look into his upward facing eyes without too much extra effort. The old man could see from his expression, that Davis was lost.

"What are you looking at?" asked Ezra.

"I'm not sure," Davis answered. "But the rain feels good on my face."

Ezra looked to the sky and felt the rain on his face. It was cold. After a few seconds of standing, letting the water run up his nose, he decided it didn't feel good on his face at all. He grabbed a hold of the lapels of Davis' jacket and tried to snap him out of his stupor.

"Okay, look ass-balls," Ezra growled at him. "You have something very important to someone I know and I have come to get it."

"Oh yeah, what do I have?" Davis asked. By now his attention had turned back skyward and it was beginning to piss Ezra off.

"A book. A stupid black and white book. Somebody I know wants it very badly and they sent me to get it." Ezra began to shout and produced the lead pipe from the bag he carried. "Now do yourself a favor and give me the bastarding thing and I won't show you how well I can play a down beat on your bastarding skull."

Davis took off his backpack and reached in without looking. He grabbed hold of the book and handed it to Ezra.

"Here," he said. "You can have it."

"Really?" Ezra asked in astonishment.

"Sure. What's the use of having power if you're not allowed to use it?" He pushed the book firmly into Ezra's hands and put his other on top of Ezra's.

"I hope it's of more use to you than it was to me," Davis said then walked down the stairs.

Ezra stood in the rain and wondered what just happened. He hadn't even raised the lead pipe against him, let alone hit him with it, but Davis Mareth was speaking like his bell had been well and truly rung. Something really was wrong with the kid and it was gnawing at Ezra's insides like a rat in a milk crate.

"Hey kid!" he called out to Davis.

Davis continued to walk silently down the concrete steps. Ezra ran after him and grabbed his shoulders.

"Davis, wait!" he said.

Davis stopped, then turned to the older man. "What do you want? You have the goddamned book now just go and leave me alone."

"I just wanted to ask you if you wanted to go get a cup of coffee or something," Ezra said.

"Isn't that a bit unusual for a mugger? To take his victim out for a hot drink after committing the crime?"

"I'm not a mugger," Ezra began. "Technically I am not mugging you because I didn't hit you. I told you I was going to rob you of your possessions, which would make me a robber. At least it would if you hadn't just given me the book." Ezra smiled at the young man and to his great surprise and relief, the young man smiled back.

"I think a coffee would be good, but in this weather, a whisky might be better," Davis said.

Davis, followed in short order by Ezra, walked through the doors of Butlers, the only tavern in town, stood on this spot at the bottom of the hill from Winterbourne Home for almost as long as the place on the top of the hill was there. It was a working man's bar then and it remained as such now. Full of people who had, long ago, given up their dreams in exchange for strong drink and ancient, greying pickled eggs.

Davis walked through the door and stood in the entrance way as his eyes adjusted to the dim lights within. Heads looked up from drinks and a chorus of murmuring struck up. As Ezra came in behind him, the murmuring was replaced by shouts of greetings toward the older man and their suspicion of the younger one vanished.

The place smelled musty and dank like an old man's basement stairs and the air hung heavy with smoke and fractured hopes. The once green carpet was adorned with a wide black stripe either from the wear of heavy traffic or someone had set it ablaze. Either was a real possibility in this place.

Ezra led the way to a booth and waited as Davis took a seat; he made his way back up to the bar, nodded and exchanged pleasantries with the patrons as he waited for the bartender. Ezra spoke to him and they both looked over to Davis. The bartender made a gesture with his hand and Ezra let go a full bellied laugh and walked back to the booth carrying a tray full of shot glasses and two bottles of beer.

"A couple of drinks?" Davis asked the older man.

"Anything worth doing, is worth doing well." Ezra smiled.

"What do you want me to do with her?" the orderly asked Nancy.

Nancy Seasons flopped her legs over the side and pushed herself up out of the bed she laid in, already covered in the girl's blood.

"Get her out of here," she ordered.

"Wait. I have something else in mind." Nancy looked up to the rafters and cracked a loathsome grin. The director had explained in detail when and how this Death ritual needed to happen, he hadn't said anything about where it had to be performed and this place seemed as good as any other. She looked at her watch, the hours ticked away and it would be sunset before she knew it. If she didn't start to prepare, midnight would come and go and she would be nothing more than she was yesterday.

"Get this bed out of here and find some rope," she said to the custodian.

He finished buttoning his shirt and headed for the door.

"And a bucket," she said and a broad, shameless smile crept onto his face.

After three shots of whisky each and too many moments of uncomfortable silence, Davis looked up at Ezra and spoke.

"What's your story?"

"You wouldn't believe me if I told you," Ezra said.

"Mr.?" Davis began.

"Ezra," Ezra finished.

"Ezra. I have seen more things up on top of that hill that I don't believe myself. I got a dollar that says anything you tell me won't even come close."

Davis could feel the liquor working on him, his temperature rose and his uneasiness was fading fast. He didn't care, he felt, even without the booze, that he would have told this man everything anyway. It was all weighing so very heavily on his soul, Nancy and Jenn and Lois and everything else he had seen since walking through the front doors of Winterbourne Home and he needed to unburden himself. There was a comfort in talking to Ezra. He gave the unmistakable impression of someone who had experienced depths of unfathomable sadness and came out the other end in spite of himself. Davis told him all of it—every detail and found that, no matter how fantastical all of it seemed, Ezra took it all in and never judged anything Davis was saying.

"What are you going to do?" Ezra asked him.

"Well, I've got to stop her, don't I?" Davis replied.

"How do you intend to do that?"

"Not a fucking clue," Davis admitted. "Any way I can, I guess."

"This kind of thing isn't as easy as all that," Ezra said, sounding suddenly very serious. "You could get killed doing this, people who want that kind of power won't give it up easily, and never without a fight."

"As long as it stopped her from going through with it, then I guess I would be all right with dying."

"Really?" Ezra eyed him suspiciously.

"Yeah, really," Davis replied, a little surprised at his own frankness. "I don't have a problem dying if it puts things right. I'm one guy, I am not going to make a difference to anything anytime soon."

Ezra nodded in silence.

"If somebody told you that you could make absolutely certain that tomorrow would be just like today for generations to come or that with one thing you could make everything right for all times if you gave up your life, wouldn't you do it? Wouldn't you think it was a fair trade?" Davis asked him.

Ezra's eyes began to well up and he put his hand in his pocket to feel for the picture. He sat silent for a long time when Davis spoke.

"Oh, hey," he said in earnest "Hey, I'm sorry. I've said something wrong. I didn't mean anything..."

"No," said Ezra. "I gave up something important a very, very long time ago because of someone's promise of wealth and security for the people I loved, it turned out to be all piss and wind. I would give my life a thousand times over if I could put things right again, even for just a minute." He buried his face in his hands.

CHAPTER 23

Davis looked to the wearied man sitting across from him, not wanting to interrupt his grief but feeling, if he did, he might be able to help him somehow. With trembling hands, he reached across the slight distance and grabbed Ezra's hand. In an instant, he got a flash of the man sitting across from him. He saw a younger man in a crisp, white uniform, picking up a small blonde haired girl and held her lovingly in his arms. The man set the blonde girl down and turned to a handsome woman who looked unimpressed and as though she might scold the man, given half a chance. He kissed her on the forehead and told her that he had a good feeling about his meeting with the director.

Then he saw the man standing in an office, listening to a balding man with glasses, who was obviously in charge of him. Davis felt the young man's knees go weak when the balding man told him what he had to do and then watched as the young man put his hand in his pocket and feel the picture in it as he walked into the room with a woman tied to a chair. Seeing the balding man walk out of the room, he then watched the younger man walk around the chair to face the woman in it. Davis saw the young man walk back behind the girl and, with trembling hands, raise the ligature.

"Jenn!" Davis shouted and yanked his hand away from Ezra's.

Ezra looked up from the table, his eyes filled with tears. Davis felt, for the first time, that this man was fully aware of what Davis was seeing and experiencing it along with him.

"I can't do...I've got to go."

Davis grabbed the book from the table beside Ezra and burst out the front door of Butler's like a Ziploc bag full of vegetable soup, bouncing and spilling as he went. He wasn't sure why he felt he needed to take the bothersome black and white book other than an inkling he might need it at some point soon. The young man staggered into the street and his head began to spin as the cold air slapped him. The younger man started drunkenly pin balling down the hill toward the bus stop to take him home but then rethought it and started slowly making his way back up the hill toward Winterbourne. Davis needed to see her. Jenn might be able to make sense of all of this. His brain was awash in a sea of old man's whisky and his thoughts kept returning to her. Having just seen the dark haired woman tied to that chair and naive hands lifting an oily length of braided rope behind her to snuff her out like a candle. He collapsed against the side of a building and vomited all over it and himself.

By the time the custodian returned to the small room, Nancy Seasons had dragged the pretty nurse's corpse from the bed to the middle of the floor. He wasn't the brightest member of the staff of Winterbourne, but it didn't take a genius to figure out what Nancy was up to. His skin crawled a little as he tied the rope around the pretty nurse's ankles. He threw the other end over the rafters and began to pull. When she was suspended sufficiently off of the floor, he tied off the rope to a coat hook on the opposite wall and looked to see that the corpse was moving like a pendulum, but not falling from its present moorings.

Nancy stood before him, completely nude and covered in the spatter and gore that resulted from the manner of the poor girl's demise. A black stripe, the width of two fingers, traversed her eyes from one temple to the other. She held in one hand a long, black handled knife with a curved, gleaming silver blade, in the other a bucket.

"You should leave now," she said without looking at him.

"Yes, Ma'am," he said to her. "If you need anything else, you know where I'll be."

"I will need you back in this room before midnight. I will have the book by then and the ritual can begin as planned. Until then, I don't need to see you, yes?"

The custodian left the small room and headed back out toward the main lobby of Winterbourne. He knew that if hung around and did as he was told, she would let him in on whatever she was up to. The thick, muscular man didn't need to know what that was, he didn't care. Nancy wasn't much to look at, and when she tried to be charming, she was even less so, but she was on her way to making a big noise in this town. If she needed a silent flunky to ask how high when she said jump, he didn't mind being the one. She would at least make it worthwhile when she allowed him to come back down again, in more ways than one. What did he care if a handful of old goats came out of Winterbourne on stretchers around the same time, it was a nursing home after all.

As he pushed through the double doors to the reception desk, he saw Davis Mareth heading into the men's room off the main hall and he carried Nancy's book.

"Son of a bitch!" he sputtered.

He looked around to see that no one noticed him following Davis inside. The custodian thought about it and smiled to himself. Who would be suspicious of two men having to pee at the same time anyway?

Davis was bent over the sink and he couldn't tell but he thought the man might be vomiting. He approached the prostrate man and squared up to him.

"You Davis Mareth?" he barked at him.

"Who wants to flow?" Davis answered.

"What?" asked the large man confused by Mareth's watery response.

"Who wants to know, you?" Davis spewed out in an angry tone.

The custodian grabbed Davis by the lapels and raised a fist the size of a side of beef. Davis closed his eyes, braced for the blow that was to come and proceeded to pass out entirely. His dead weight slid out of the orderly's hands and to the floor like 160-pound bag of slugs. He stood confused, completely unsure what he should do next and then somewhere, deep in seldom visited parts of his brain, a naked bulb hanging from the ceiling flickered on and revealed an easel with a piece of paper on it that read, Grab The Book. The orderly did, then left the bathroom with it under his arm and headed back to the small room to give the book over to Nancy. Hoping just a little that she would be in the middle of whatever she was doing and would have worked herself into a frenzy and would need him to help her relax.

When Davis woke, his head was in Jenn's lap again and she was rubbing his forehead with a cold damp cloth.

"Oh my God," he said, "my head feels like it's going to come off."

"And he didn't even hit you," Jenn giggled.

He sat himself upright and hugged her, grabbing her as though he might never see her again if he let go of her. The thought of what he had seen pushing aside the feeling of joy he had for just seeing her again.

"I'm so sorry." He tried to pull away to look at her face.

"Why?" She pulled him in closer and kissed his forehead. "You didn't do it."

"But I sat there with him, I got drunk with him and I began to like him. Even after I saw all of that, I still feel a little sorry for him."

"You should," Jenn said. "He is not the one to blame for this, Ezra was pushed by someone who used the love of his child against him, and he did something horrific because he felt he had no other choice."

"He killed you, Jenn!" Davis yelled. "Doesn't that mean anything to you?"

"Of course it does," Jenn answered.

"What?" Davis asked, dubious of what she had just said.

"It means Ezra helped me meet you."

"How is that even possible?' he asked her.

"Davis Mareth, I was born a very long time ago, I suspect years before your grandmamma even. If Ezra hadn't done what he did, I likely would have led a very tedious, stodgy life, got old and died naturally long before you were ever born. If Ezra hadn't killed me," she laughed, "I wouldn't be here."

Davis thought about this for a moment and began to see the logic in it. As twisted as it may seem, she was dead right. If she hadn't been murdered, she'd have been long dead.

"You said somebody else pushed Ezra into killing you, right?"

"Yes," Jenn answered hesitantly.

"Did you know who was responsible? Did the big D?" Davis asked.

"Of course he did, it's his job to know these things."

"And he didn't stop it?" Davis asked with growing ire.

"He couldn't have even if he wanted to. I thought you got this part?" she asked.

"I do but…"

"But what, Davis. Spit it out?" Jenn demanded.

"Why is Ezra still here?" Davis asked.

She thought for a moment before answering.

"I can't tell you that. I mean I can but it's best to hear it from the source."

She reached in to hug him and he leaned his head to kiss her. She pushed him away.

"Why is it you always want to kiss me when you have puke breath?"

Davis blushed and hugged her tightly.

"Look," she said. "I want you to go see Lois. She isn't doing well and might enjoy the visit."

"She's awake?" Davis asked hopefully.

"No," said Jenn. "But it doesn't mean that she doesn't know you're there. She could certainly use the company."

"I'll go now," Davis said.

She held him again and pulled him so tight; he felt the wind being pushed out of him a little.

"Things are going to happen soon, wondrous, terrible things and you will be forced to make a decision. It won't be an easy one, decide with your heart and you will make the right choice."

"What is the right choice?" Davis asked her.

"Only you know the answer to that."

She let him go then walked out of the bathroom.

He knew what she meant and he had been cringing at the thought of it since he was with her in the unfinished office. Davis stood up and walked to the sink, he was still a little lightheaded from going toe to toe with Ezra and his bottle of Old Grand-dad and his mouth tasted like the inside of a birdcage. It's no wonder she didn't want to kiss him. He threw cold water up in his face, several times and filled his mouth with water. Still no good, so he stuck his head completely under the tap and turned the cold water on full. After more than a couple of minutes, Davis looked up and felt some of the whisky inside his brain being replaced with actual blood.

The young man looked at himself in the mirror and wished he had a comb or a towel at least. His face was pale and sallow, though his eyes were still the same brilliant, electric neon whorehouse shade of blue. Davis thought of the old expression and laughed to himself because, for all intents and purposes, not only did he look it, he was Death warmed over. He shook as much water off his hair as possible and ran his hands through it in a makeshift, combing motion then headed to Lois' room.

Davis stood outside of her room, almost afraid to go in when he got the strangest sensation that something was not right inside. He elbowed the door open and hurried in, only to be stopped dead. Three of the wild Rastafarian, chimpanzee things circled the bed Lois laid unconscious on. The largest of the three jumped up on the bed and was heading for her face, fangs bared and claws at the ready.

Without thinking, Davis grabbed the thing on Lois' bed by the throat then hurled it against the wall. The other two rounded on him, hissing and scraping their long claws against the floor as they charged. In a heartbeat, they were standing on top of his chest, digging their claws into his flesh. Davis could feel the heat of their breath. They stank of decay. Davis wretched. One of them raised its wicked, clawed hand and wrapped it around Davis' throat. It wasn't long before Davis felt the blood trickle down his neck. The lights in the room dimmed.

The whistling sound came from the largest of the three and it caused the thing, currently trying to strangle Davis Mareth, to momentarily loosen its grip. It turned toward the sound.

"Sorry chaps," said the largest thing. "This one's not for us."

The two things on top of Davis stood and rushed to stand alongside the largest one. They began to speak amongst themselves in a series of grunts and snorts and wild hand gestures. The largest thing put up its clawed hands in a calming gesture and the two smaller ones lowered their heads in obvious disappointment. They walked toward the closet door. The largest thing turned to him and spoke, in the accent he had heard in his dream.

"Dreadfully sorry old Guillemot, honest mistake and all, you understand don't you? There's a good chap."

It walked toward the closet with the others and Davis could see a light begin to rise up from the floor inside the closet. The door opened slowly and the room was bathed in the same golden light Davis saw the night old Arthur Gordon died. The three grim, ape things walked into the closet and the door began to close after them. The tallest of the three glanced at Davis with a look that was both knowing and taunting at the same time. Without much conscious effort, Davis shot his foot out and came to rest between the closing door and the jamb. He pulled the closet door open and slipped inside, hoping to avoid the things who had gone in before him. They were nowhere to be seen and the familiarity of this place hadn't changed, it was exactly as he had dreamed it.

Davis Mareth stood at the base of a gigantic set of stone stairs, identical to the ones he saw in his dream. He could smell the same ancient must and mildew as before and the steps still looked moss covered and slippery as they had in the dream. Looking toward the top of the circular staircase, his eyes met with complete darkness. Cautiously, he grabbed a torch from a sconce on the wall and put his foot on the first step, took a deep breath and started to climb the staircase.

CHAPTER 24

Nancy Seasons stood in the middle of a small, plain room that wasn't much bigger than a prison cell and about as welcoming. The walls were white washed cinderblocks loosely covered in sheets of blood flecked tarpaulin. It was cold and unwelcoming and perfectly placed for doing as she please to whom she pleased without attracting any attention

"Where did this come from?" Nancy Seasons asked suspiciously.

The heavyset custodian told her the story of Davis Mareth passing out in the men's room.

"I just took it from him," he said with the glee of a small boy. "I didn't have to hit him or nothing; I just picked it up from the floor."

He passed her the book and she jerked it away from him like an angry mother pulling a crying child from the toy aisle of a department store.

"Where is Mareth now?" she seethed.

"Still in the bathroom, I guess," he answered her.

He lowered his head to avoid her gaze. The big man saw Nancy like this once before and it made the fear creep up through him like a python. If Nancy Seasons didn't get exactly what she wanted when she wanted, all hell would break loose and the people standing closest to her when she let loose, would be the first to go.

"I told you we needed him here, yes?" Her tone changed, drastically. She went from unimaginable anger to sickly sweet, dulcet tones. The custodian began to stutter in a blind panic of what was coming from her next.

"I…I was just so excited to get the book, I wanted to get back here and give it to you as soon as I could."

He could sense she was about to explode and he was standing in the center of ground zero holding a great big daisy. Nancy closed her eyes and took the deepest breath he'd ever seen anyone take. When the last of it had been expelled slowly and forcefully, through tightly pursed lips, she opened her reptilian eyes and looked right through him.

"No matter," she breathed in the same terrifying, placating voice. "In time he will come here and then you will hold him while I cut his throat and watch the last hope of a balance between the living and the dead spill away with every ambrosial, crimson drop that comes out of him."

The custodian swallowed hard and took a step back, fully expecting her to lash out at him in some way. When it didn't come, he felt like he should get down on hand and knee and thank her for keeping him around for one more day. He didn't but he managed a tongue-tied "thank-you, Ma'am" and waited for her to tell him what to do next.

Nancy opened the black and white composition book and after examining it for a time, she looked around the room and moved toward the bucket beneath the young nurse's dangling corpse. She looked up to the young girl and motioned to her accomplice.

"Cut this thing down and get it out of here," she smiled a wicked smile. "And then come right back here with two paint brushes, we've got work to do."

Ezra Schneider looked up from his eighth straight whisky. It had been two hours since Davis Mareth left Butler's. In the normal run of things he would have written him off the second he stood up. He offered him a couple of drinks and a little solace in the midst of an unbelievably shitty day. If he didn't want it, that was his problem, not Ezra's. But this was not the normal run of things, not by a long shot. He stood, made his peace with the bartender and headed out to the street. The old man thought he could probably walk to his car but in the same amount of time, he could probably make it up the hill on his own power. The walk would do him good anyway.

The cold air felt good against the rising heat of the whisky in his head. He stood outside Butler's and let the mist and cold air pour all over him. Ezra stretched out his arms and raised his face to the heavens. He would never admit it but maybe the kid was on to something, it did feel pretty good. A passerby eyed him up, like he was some wild eyed drunk in the throes of a staggering bacchanalia and made a wide sweeping arc to get by him without any risk of coming into contact with him. The intent of the motion was not lost on the old man.

"Oh yeah?" he hollered out. "Oh yeah, just walk by piss bag. This is none of your assing business anyway."

Ezra adjusted his coat, pulled the collar up around his neck and headed up the hill, muttering all along the way.

"This bastarding town can just kiss my balls from now on," he groused.

A plump mother had just come out of Cruickshank's department store and pulled her daughter up away from the shabby-looking man talking to himself.

"Goddamn people in this town," he muttered, keeping his eyes firmly fixed on the ground as he walked by.

Ezra wasn't quite sure why Davis walked out in such a rush but he had a pretty good idea. Being alive for 115 years, he had come across a handful of people who could do things that defied belief. Some could look at you and know you were lying before a single word left your lips and some could ask your name as you bought them a drink and tell everything about you before the ice cubes were rattling in the glass. He figured Davis fell in somewhere between the two. Ezra couldn't explain why but he knew that his life and Davis Mareth's were irrevocably intertwined and now his destiny lie along the same road as this young man's.

He made it to the steps of Winterbourne and hesitated before he went up them. Ezra took the picture out of his pocket and kissed the little girl's image.

"One more time, Baby?" he asked the little blonde girl, "and then Daddy's coming home, for good."

He made his way through the front doors and stood by the reception desk, undecided about what he should do next. Ezra had to find Davis but he wasn't even certain he was here. The old man stood frozen, looking from one side of the big room to the other.

"Can I help you sir?" the girl behind the reception desk asked Ezra.

"You can mind your own bastarding business, Miss nosey assing Parker" was on the tip of his tongue, screaming to leap out at the young girl.

Ezra thought that perhaps this particular time in his life might require a more delicate approach. If the receptionist thought him a helpless old fool, she might be more inclined to help him out. So he padded over to the desk and tried to use his best hangdog expression, to make himself seem as helpless as possible.

"I was to meet my nephew here, to get a good look at the place. I think I'll be moving in here before next winter and I wanted to have a look around the place, you see?"

"Oh, okay," said the receptionist a little confused. "And is your nephew…um… here already?"

"My heavens, ha, ha," Ezra said, pouring it on syrupy thick. "No, no, my dear, he doesn't live here, he works here."

"Oh," she said as though she made a gigantic breakthrough. "That should be easy then. What is your nephew's name?"

"Davis Mareth," said Ezra.

"Oh yeah?" said the receptionist. "I know him. I saw him come in but I don't see him signed in yet. He might be in a meeting or something. Would you like me to page him?"

"That would be just swell," said Ezra.

He reached across the desk and lightly pinched the young woman's cheek as he winked at her. The young woman blushed and called the page over the loudspeaker.

"Davis Mareth to reception please, Davis Mareth to reception."

"There are a few chairs over there if you'd like to sit and wait," the receptionist suggested.

"That would be lovely, young lady," Ezra answered, a little nauseated by the candied pleasantness rolling so easily off his tongue.

He shuffled his way over to the chairs and sat slowly down in one, huffing and puffing as he went. The old man hated to pour it on this thick but reasoned that calling the woman ass balls and telling her to fetch Davis bastarding Mareth was going to get him nowhere. The reception area was a sprawling and slightly overwhelming place with a large L shaped desk at the center of it. To the left and right of the desk stood doorways to an unfinished hallway and the resident wards. From the seating area in front of the desk he had a clear view of the entire reception area, and so when the big custodian came around the corner after hearing the page, Ezra saw him long before he even got close to reception desk.

"What's that big bastard doing here?"

Ezra recognized him as one of the two orderlies who had helped to lure him down this dark path long, long ago. The old man felt his blood begin to boil and he wanted to rush the man and beat him senseless. He wouldn't need to move far, as the orderly noticed Ezra, he began to move directly to him. When he reached him, the orderly grabbed Ezra around the arm and leaned in to him.

"Still looking around for that bastard kid of yours, old man?" he hissed.

"Mark my words," Ezra said coolly. "I will pull your eyes out and piss on your brain before all of this is over."

"Pretty tough talk for a man of your advanced age," The orderly said. "I got somebody who wants to see you."

"I'm not gonna be part of this shit again," Ezra spat. "I really am not."

"We'll see," said the orderly.

He looked to the receptionist whose expression was one of a person about to call the police.

"Mr. Schneider is out of his ward again, I need to get him back now," the orderly said to the young girl behind the desk.

The receptionist returned to mindlessly leafing through the magazine on her desk. The less she knew the better, she thought.

The orderly led Ezra toward the unfinished hallway and in through the double doors.

"I'm too old for all of this strong-arm shit and so are you," Ezra said. "Let go of me and just point me in the right direction, I'm through running."

To Ezra's surprise, the beefy custodian let go of his arm. They walked on together toward the small room where Nancy was preparing. The orderly looked over at Ezra and spoke, "Would it mean anything to you if I said I was sorry?"

"Depends," Ezra stated. "Would you mean it if you said it?"

"I might," said the ham-fisted orderly.

"It might, then," Ezra replied.

The orderly stopped in front of a small white door and pushed it open.

"Inside," he said.

The walls were covered in symbols large and small, arcane and eldritch and written in what looked like fresh blood. In the center of the floor was a symbol that spanned nearly the width of the entire room, also written in blood. At the center of the circle with her back to the door, stood Nancy Seasons, completely nude and covered from head to toe in the same symbols that adorned the room, though these figures had been carved deep into her flesh and she was dripping blood from each one of them.

Ezra walked through the door and stared at Nancy in disbelief, he knew she was desperate but this went far beyond anything he thought her capable of.

She turned as the two men entered the room, expecting to see the orderly alone; she was surprised to see Ezra standing there with him, though her face betrayed no such shock.

"What's this?" she cooed at Ezra. "An unexpected guest? How delightful. There's always room for one more." The words trickled off her lips like a parent whose child has brought a friend home for dinner without asking, not like a woman who was trying to upset the fabric of reality.

"Put some clothes on you fat evil sow," Ezra said.

The orderly snickered. She spun and stared him down. Her eyes changed as quickly as the tone of her voice. They weren't dull brown anymore, they weren't even human. They glistened the color as the bloody symbols that covered her body and to all appearances, the blood flowed through them, out of them and back in again like a grisly, sanguineous fountain.

"SILENCE!" she shrieked at him in a voice that made his heart shake in terrible desperation. Nancy raised a hand in front of him and he felt his feet leaving the floor. She waved her hand deliberately toward the front of the room, as though she were shooing a fly away from a slice of cake and his body slammed hard against the whitewashed stone wall. The big orderly went limp and hit the floor. She turned the bloody fountains to Ezra and spoke with a voice that was both Nancy Seasons and the man who once forced him to kill.

"Now, my old friend," the Nancy horror croaked. "Let's chat, yes?"

CHAPTER 25

Davis didn't remember the stairs being quite this long or hard to climb in the dream. They seemed to be sweating with all of the condensation on them, and it made the footing difficult, to say the least. Walking up them was like climbing Everest in tennis shoes. He had to stop every five or six steps to catch his breath. It was beginning to feel like he would never reach the top and he was nearly to the point where he didn't care if he made it or not.

"Better late than never," Davis said.

He became aware there were hundreds of pairs of eyes watching him as he ascended the stairs and every now and then he would catch quick bursts of movement out of the corners of his eyes. Davis felt like there were many things intently watching his every move, observing him tire and need more and more rest the higher he got on the staircase that seemed never ending. It also felt like if he stopped for more than a few minutes, they would descend on him and rip him to shreds. He waved his torch into the blackness that surrounded him, but nothing was exposed by the arcing light. Undaunted, he felt for the wall of the staircase and continued upward.

Davis stopped again after a few steps and swung the torch around. It caught one of the Rastafarian chimpanzee things and sent it scrambling off into the darkness, yowling like a scalded dog.

"Anyone else want to play?" Davis shouted to the darkness.

He heard the same grunts and snorts and clicks he heard in Lois's room. They seemed to be discussing things amongst themselves and by the sound of it, had come to some sort of agreement.

"Well?" Davis called out.

"We're just reasoning things out, dear boy, won't be a moment."

Davis recognized the voice of the large thing.

After a few minutes of not hearing the grunts and clicks anymore, Davis called out to them.

"What's the story?"

"Sorry, old bean," the large thing called out. "I've asked around and it seems the lads are...well, entirely resolved to rend the flesh from your bones and satiate themselves on your innards in glut of violence and bloodshed. Nothing personal, mind."

Davis thought if he ran quickly enough, he might be able to keep ahead of them until he got back to the bottom of the staircase. But if he fell, or if his lungs gave out and he had to stop to get his breath, he was done for. He remembered the confrontation with these things in Lois' room and, though he was sure there were many more now, he convinced himself that it was time to stand his ground. Determined to make a stand, he put his back to the wall of the staircase and held his torch out in front of him.

"Come ahead," Davis called out to the things.

It wasn't long before the first one showed up. Small and quick, it dodged the first swipe of Davis' torch and leaped toward his face but Davis' reflexes seemed suddenly, otherworldly and he dodged it completely. The speed it was traveling and the dead stop against the wall behind Davis knocked it out cold, but there were more to replace it and they were coming in twos and threes. Davis swung his torch like a sword and cut several of them down with one fiery sweep. He was amazed that the impact of the torch against their scaly mottled skin didn't put the torch out altogether, but the more they came and the more he swung, the brighter the thing seemed to burn. Wave after wave the wild simian things set in on him and he bashed them with torch and fist and foot until he thought he might collapse from exhaustion. It was then he saw the big thing walking toward him with a chain in its hand. At the end of that chain, about a foot behind it, was a gigantic thing, nearly the height of Davis. It was identical to all the other Rastafarian chimpanzee things save for its size and the monstrous tusks jutting from its jaws. Compared to the others, it was a behemoth.

The big thing looked stupid and mean and, though its eyes were closed, the brute did not look as though it was fond of communicating beyond brute force and blunt savagery. Davis made a move to a higher step, to the higher ground and the thing's eyes snapped open, zeroing in on Davis' eyes. It snorted at the air and pulled at its chain, moving toward Davis, claws extended from thick, club-like digits. The smaller thing tugged back at the chain and the brute stopped its advance, for the moment.

"C'mon you bastard!" Davis screamed at the gruesome pair.

"My dear boy," the smaller of the two looked up and said, "you can't possibly come out of this unmarred. You are well and proper conquered. Now if you could just put down the torch and lay sort of prostrate in front of my large friend here, we can get on with it. All right?"

Davis thought for a second. He was just tired enough that the suggestion of laying down was unbelievably appealing to him and he was tempted to give in. It wasn't much farther to go before he reached the top of the stairs and the thought of giving in to this smug little bastard made him feel like he needed shower.

"Sorry, old egg," Davis mocked. "Not much in the mood for dying today, I'm afraid. Nothing personal, you see?"

Davis pushed his back against the wall of the staircase and gripped the torch tightly in both hands. The smaller thing closed in and stepped full into the circle of the torch light, tugging the frightening, giant thing behind it.

"No, *I'm* sorry, old egg," it wheezed and its eyes narrowed on Davis. "But this is going to be extremely painful."

It dropped the chain.

Davis closed his eyes as the monstrous dreadlocked, primate bounded toward him. He felt the hot, rank breath long before it was near enough to smell. He turned his head sideways and braced for the impact he knew was going to bring about a quick and painless end, but it didn't arrive. Instead he got the sensation of a very large bright light shining down on his face.

He opened his eyes and turned his head from the very bright light that shone in his face. Davis saw that both of the things were gone now and with his strength somewhat renewed by the light, he headed up the last few stairs.

When he reached the top, Davis was surprised to find it was not like his dream at all. There was a desk whose occupant was seated with his back to the stairs. The rest of the room looked less like a castle and more like the living room of an old woman's house, if the woman was colorblind and had lived alone all of her life.

There was furniture, of a type, covered in plastic and didn't look very comfortable, so that even if it weren't covered, Davis would be hesitant to sit on any of it. There were windows up here, wrapped in lace curtains which were topped with vast, gaudy, valances. They looked like someone had rolled a plaid blanket in melted wax and stuck it to the top of the window. A shabby table, with four shabby chairs around it sat in the center of the room with lace settings at either end of. A big console television sat along the far wall of the room and a console stereo on the other. If Davis didn't know better, he would have thought he stepped into the props department of *I Love Lucy*. The only thing that didn't fit with the impossibly bizarre décor, but tying it all together in total strangeness nonetheless, were the cats. They had infiltrated everywhere. Black ones with great yellow eyes and white ones with eyes nearly as blue as Davis'. Calicos and Siamese, Scottish folds and Sphinx, there were hundreds of them and the stench made his eyes water the closer he got.

The stench failed to dissuade his curiosity and he moved closer to the figure at the desk.

"I've been waiting, Davis," the figure said. "It's been a very long time."

Davis walked forward, inching closer to the desk; terribly nervous about what he would find when he was finally face to face with the figure in the chair. When he got to the high-backed chair, he reached out with apprehensive, outstretched fingers and felt the suppleness of the leather in his hand. He took a firm hold of it and turned it around.

The young man had been through many things in his life. He was an orphan and had been raised by a long list of people that cared more about the results of scratch tickets and fruit machines than they did about him and the nightmares that plagued him. He saw people torn to shreds by child-sized chimpanzee, porcupine Chupacabra-looking things. And people kissed away by beautiful, impossibly small boys with delicate black wings and the whispers of love eternal on their perfect pink lips. Yet despite all that, nothing prepared him for what was in the leather chair as he turned it around.

"Not quite what you were expecting?" asked Bob Newhart.

CHAPTER 26

The bloody horror that was Nancy threw the book at Ezra and commanded him to read.

"I can't read this junk," Ezra said. "It's not even English."

He tossed the book back at her and Nancy shot a blood-filled look at the book. It stopped in midair and dropped before her. She meandered toward Ezra in a series of jerky, broken movements. Soon the bloody pools were looking into Ezra's eyes. She lifted her hand and Ezra lifted off the ground; then waved her hand slowly and he came to rest on a small chair near the crumpled form of the orderly.

"Have a seat," she said.

There was a rattle in her voice that sounded like she had a monstrous head cold and her throat was packed up with phlegm.

"I don't want to sit in any bastarding chairs just now, thank you," Ezra said and attempted to get up. He couldn't move.

"Problems?" Nancy rasped.

"None at all," Ezra returned.

She waved her hands again and Ezra felt a weight tighten around his wrists, as if the arms of the chairs had become pythons and they were constricting themselves around his arms in hopes of a quick meal. Nancy wiggled her fingers in a mock come hither gesture and Ezra felt his fingers begin to curl back toward the tops of his wrists until he felt his fingernails touch his watch. Ezra strained against the pressure of this affront to his body and just as he thought his wrists might snap entirely, she stopped. His wrists returned to their normal, fingernails up position. She moved her hand again and the book flew into Ezra's lap.

"Try to follow along, yes?" She gurgled and glided to the center of the bloody symbol on the floor.

"Yn awr yn dod I mi Marwolaeth mawr."

The words echoed through the small room and Ezra felt a rumble from deep within the recesses of Winterbourne.

"Dewch yn awr, yn dod yn awr ac yn sefyll ger fy mron eich meistr!"

The room began to shake and flakes of paint and dust began to fall from the ceiling like a macabre snow fall. The rumbling grew deeper and

S. A. BAKER

fissures began to open along the walls, oozing shafts of greasy blue light.

"Oh Marwolaeth, fwytawr mawr o fyd, yn dod yn awr ac ymgrymu i mi!"

As the words left her lips, the blue light became stronger and brighter and the beams focused on her. Nancy Seasons rose into the air and Ezra Schneider could hear a sound like a gigantic dynamo coming to life and beginning its steady low drone. She began to spin, bathed in the greasy blue light, round and round at withering speed. Ezra heard Nancy scream and thought she was being ripped apart by the centrifugal forces of the dizzying spiral. As suddenly as it began, the whirlwind stopped and Nancy hung in midair. Contorted and distorted into unnatural positions, she screamed and cried out for it to stop. The voice was no longer the gurgling, gagging mixture of Nancy and The Director. It was all Nancy Seasons now and it was terrified.

"Please," she cried out. "Please I don't want it, I don't want it!"

The more she pleaded, the worse the contortions became. As she shrieked, she was twisted by unseen, malevolent hands until at last she was folded nearly in half then fainted. The contortions stopped and she dropped to the floor in the middle of the blood symbol.

Ezra felt whatever bonds were holding him to the chair release, and he walked over to Nancy's deflated body.

"Not even you deserved that," Ezra said quietly to her.

Her eyes snapped open, the blood had all but disappeared and they were now the greasy blue color of the light streaming through the walls. She rose up to a sickening crunch of bone as she moved each limb and joint of her body. The Nancy thing jerked and cracked her head from side to side as she trained her eyes on him. A voice that dripped with an evil beyond words and made his soul hurt just to hear it.

"Yn awr yr wyf yn dod yn Marwolaeth, ddistryw o fydoedd."

She reached out a boney finger and touched Ezra, almost delicately, on the forehead. He dropped like a stone and all went black.

CHAPTER 27

"You're him?" Davis asked.

"Uh huh," Bob Newhart answered. "I am the Great Leveler, The…ah…Servant of the Void."

Davis stood, mouth agape, unable to believe what and who he was looking at.

"I know," said Bob Newhart. "You were expecting the black robe and the scythe, right?"

"You're not even a skeleton," Davis remarked.

"No, but I could be. I can be anything, to anyone. I am entirely subjective, just like Death. Which ah…is me."

"I have no idea what to say right now," Davis confided.

"I'm going to be honest with you," Death began. "There are many aspects of this job that don't make a lot of sense. You just, sort of learn to go along with them."

He took a deep breath and his face began to shimmer like a pool of mercury. Soon Bob Newhart was gone, replaced by the familiar visage of a very skeletal death.

"Is…is this better?"

"The look is better," said Davis. "But the voice is still a little off."

"The big hollow voice takes a few days to get going. This is the best I can do on short notice."

"Fine," said Davis, "go back to the man in the sweater."

His face shimmered again and Bob Newhart was back.

"Have a seat, you must have a lot of questions," Death asked. "I have the answers…well, most of them anyway."

Davis sat in the chair in front of the desk and faced Bob Newhart. His brain was packed full of questions to ask and he sat still for a long time deciding which the best question to ask first. He stared at his feet and walls, he stared at the cats on the desk and shooed the ones away that were rubbing against his legs, but his mind remained a swirl of unfocused inquiry. *What's the worst that could happen if I don't ask him anything?*

"Why me?" Davis asked Death.

Bob Newhart leaned back, rubbed his chin and took a deep breath. He let it out slowly and looked around the room. The lights began to dim and soon the only light by which they both could see were the two torches in their sconces at either end of the room.

"No," Death said, "no that's no good either."

He pushed away from the desk and took another deep breath. The lamps in the room suddenly illuminated again. He scrutinized Davis for a moment and smiled. There was warmth in that smile and Davis began to feel a little more relaxed about this whole situation in general.

"You know," Bob Newhart began, "I asked the same question many, many years ago and I'm going to tell you the same thing I was told."

Davis leaned in, expecting a staggering pearl of wisdom or some laser pointed insight as to why he was involved in any of this at all.

"The short answer," said Death, "is why not you?"

"Um, what's the long answer?" Davis asked.

"Well…ah…" Bob Newhart stammered, "How much do you remember of your mother?"

"I don't remember anything of her," Davis said with agitation. "She left me right after I was born."

"She left you," said Death, "but not like you think she did. What if I told you I was there the night you were born?"

"You were there when I was born?" Davis asked incredulously.

"In a manner of speaking, I was guiding hands and things."

"What?" said Davis.

"Your mother died in a car accident, she was hit by a car driven by the man who impregnated her."

"That's a little ironic, wouldn't you say?" Davis scarcely believed what he was heard.

"I would say it was incredibly ironic," Death pushed some papers aside. "If I weren't guiding all of it, from the night you were created to the second she died. I was there in the form of the man responsible."

"Are you telling me you are my father?" Davis was surprised at the question but wanted the answer just the same.

"Well, no," Death said, "and yes. When you take this job…ah…when you take the robe and the scythe, you give up all of that."

"All of what?" Davis asked.

Death stared at Davis as if he had asked, 'they call it jam because the jars are so full?'

"Do you…ah, do you know where babies come from, son?"

"Of course," sighed Davis.

"You give that up. But I pushed that man to your mother and I put him in the car that plowed into her and I was standing over his shoulder as he delivered you just a moment before your mother died."

"Wait, what?" asked Davis. "You mean you changed the course of things, like I wanted to do for Lois? Like Jenn told me I wasn't allowed to do, though she couldn't tell me why."

"No," said Bob Newhart. "I didn't alter the course of things; I made certain the things went the way they were meant to."

"How can you say that?" Davis asked with a wounded tone in his voice. "My mother is dead because you changed the course of her life. I didn't ever get to meet my mother because of what you did."

"What I did," Death explained, "was to make absolutely certain your mother fulfilled her role."

"Her what?" Davis spat.

"Davis, look," Death said. "You are going to find out a few things you never knew before in this job. One of them is that all of us have a role, a preset task and once we have accomplished that, the clock starts ticking down."

"What clock?" asked a disinterested Davis, thinking it was all a metaphor anyway.

"The clock of your life," said Death. "We all have a clock, you, me, all of us. It's like a time clock at work. You punch in the day you are born and once you have fulfilled your role, it's time to go home. You might get a little overtime but never enough to make a big difference. Your mother's role was to give birth to you. After she did that, her days became measured in minutes. All I did was give her a nudge in the right direction. I knocked over a purse if I remember."

"How is that any different from what I wanted to do for Lois?"

"You weren't going to help her along her way; you were trying to give her more time. You can't," said Death. "We all have a finite amount of it and when it's up, it's up."

"But that's not fair," Davis protested.

"No," said Bob Newhart. "It isn't, but Death isn't fair. Death just is. I...I know it is a tough pill to swallow at first."

"What if I don't want it?" Davis asked. "What if I say no to all of it?"

"You could," said Death. "But then the natural balance would suffer and all of the people, including your Lois, who were supposed to die, would be left here. Neither living nor dead—not going anywhere. Would Lois want to spend all of eternity trapped in Winterbourne? Would you, could you, allow that to happen to her if you could do something to stop it from happening?"

Davis turned in his chair, unable to look at Bob Newhart anymore. It was too much to take in. Too much responsibility. He could barely get out of his apartment in the morning, let alone usher souls into the great beyond with any sense of immediacy.

The large, muscular orderly closed the board and batten door, leaving the cinderblock room and the thing that was Nancy Seasons behind him. He looked at his watch, it was just past 10:30 A.M. on Wednesday and Mrs. Morrison would be waiting for him. She didn't like to be kept waiting at the best of times but on a Wednesday, their day, it was out of the question.

The big man ran a comb through his hair and hurriedly stepped on the elevator to get to the old woman's floor.

"I was beginning to think you had forgotten me," said the small woman in the wheelchair."

"I'm sorry Mrs. Morrison," said the orderly. "I was with the Director cleaning up a mess. I'm here now and we can go if you like."

The old woman gave him a sideways look.

"Very well, Kevin," she said. "I suppose we can go."

The walked together in silence for a while, the orderly pushing her silently and pretending to be remorseful for being late and the old woman not saying a word and feigning indignation at his being late again.

"I'm glad to see you, Kevin," Mrs. Morrison said.

"Really," he gasped. "I'll bet you'd be glad to see anything about now."

"Oh you," she laughed. "You're lucky I can't see or you'd have to move back under that bridge and resume frightening goats."

It was their ritual; he would come to get the old woman every Wednesday at a little after ten and the two of them would go along exchanging barbs as they walked to the only decent garden left at the back of the old estate.

"Where shall we go today? Paris, the Mediterranean? Perhaps

Pocatello? I hear the grunion are running full and fast this time of year."

"You know where I want to go," said Mrs. Morrison.

The walked leisurely along the slightly overgrown brick path to a small reflecting pool near the back corner of the grounds. And when they came to a spot where the sunlight felt warm on her face and the marigolds were close enough for her to smell but not overpower everything, they stopped.

Kevin the orderly plucked the old woman from her chair with a gentility and ease that belied his mountainous size. He produced two generous corn muffins and a small silver flask. As the old, blind woman nibbled at the muffin he gave her, he opened the lid on the flask and passed it to her.

"I don't care how drunk you get me," she said. "I'm not going home with you."

She put the flask to her lips and took the tiniest until she appreciated the truth of what was in it and then took several large swallows of its contents.

"Slow down," said Kevin. ""They're gonna fire me if I bring you back loaded."

"Get ready to lose your job," said Mrs. Morrison.

After one more longish sip, the alcohol settled itself firmly in the center of her head and soon the old woman was laughing in a carefree way like she did when she looked at her life thorough a windshield instead of a rear view mirror. She reached out for the orderly's hand.

"This is a good day," she said.

Kevin the orderly picked her up from the ground and placed her gingerly back in her chair. They walked for a short distance and he gave the flask to Mrs. Morrison one last time.

"I probably won't happen again," he said. "Better make the most of it."

"My head will pound tomorrow," the old woman said.

"Remember me when it does," Kevin said.

He pushed her chair through the doors of the big building and began to hum something stale and simple as they waited for the elevator. Mrs. Morrison seemed to recognize the tune and soon they were both humming it, even after they stepped off the lift.

"Smells funny," said the old woman.

"They're cleaning the carpets," said the orderly. "It always smells like that when they clean them."

"It's musty," she said. "Dank."

"It's very old carpet and very old smells live deep inside it."

The orderly wheeled her up to the door and bent down to face her.

"Somebody will be along to help you soon," he said and squeezed her hand tenderly.

Kevin moved her chair into the room and quietly pulled the door closed.

"Smells sweet in here," said Mrs. Morrison. "Like wilted roses."

"Yn Gwaed, ceir pwer." The Nancy Seasons thing hissed as it shambled up to the old woman and began to rend her flesh. Piece by agonizing piece.

Outside the door, Kevin the orderly stood waiting for the old woman's screaming and the high pitched, wails of blood lust to end before re-opening the door.

This is a good day, he thought.

Bob Newhart sighed. "Look, I was where you are now when I started this thing too. I didn't see the point of any of it. When the robe and scythe were offered to me, I turned them down and went home."

"But you're here," said Davis. "You're here now."

"I am," said Death, "because just being offered the job had changed me. I could see the clock above the heads of everyone I passed on the way home. My mother was standing in the doorway when I got home and I saw the clock above her head. She had less than one full day left. She was so frightened of dying her whole life, so very, very scared. I swore to my mother that I would be with her until the end and that I would make sure that she didn't suffer. The only way I could really guarantee that was to accept the offer that was put before me. I went back to the place I came from, a building much like this and told my predecessor that I accepted his offer. I went home and ushered my dear mother out of this life and I have never looked back."

"You haven't really answered my question," Davis said.

"But I have," said Bob Newhart. "Death is the great leveler, the great equalizer. There are those who face death head on, kicking and screaming and you will have them ripped away from this world and then there are people who are so frightened of the inevitability of the end that you must hold their hands and rub their backs until they are calm enough to leave. To us, there is no difference between the two. They both deserve to have a death best suited to them. That is what it is to be Death. We do not judge, condemn nor discriminate.

Davis stood up and began to walk around the room, taking it all in. His head swam in the information that was just crammed into it.

"What about the boy, the one with the black wings, is that us too?"

"You've seen him?" Bob Newhart asked. "You should consider yourself fortunate. I have only ever met him once and it was when he told me my time was running out."

"Who is he? Isn't he us?" Davis asked.

"If Death is the CEO, he is the company we work for. Beyond that, I don't know much about him. I expect you might be seeing him again if he has taken an interest in you this early."

Davis paced around the room, sighing heavily as he took each deliberate step.

"I don't know if I can do this," he said to Bob Newhart. "What happens after somebody dies? What do we do then?"

"*We* don't anything," said Death. "Do you remember the very small, particularly nasty looking things you have seen around, usually ripping someone to shreds?"

"How could anybody forget those goddamned things?"

"And do you remember a dream you had where there were many of them working in a big office?"

"I remember," said Davis.

"It wasn't...wasn't exactly a dream. It was more of a guided tour. They are the Necrosites. They are the indentured to the office of Death. They serve the robe and scythe and part of their role is to guide souls along to where they need to go. The room you saw that looked like a big waiting room was a...um... big waiting room. That's why people were angry when you got out of it right away. Some people have been in there for eons, waiting their turn. There's a bit of a backlog. Several thousand years, last time I looked."

"But they ripped Mrs. Nesbitt to pieces. I was there, I saw it."

"They were natural hunters before one of the first Deaths put them to work. It only seemed natural to continue to use them when a gruesome death is required."

"What could old Mrs. Nesbitt have possibly done to deserve that?" Davis asked.

"She didn't do anything," said Bob Newhart. "Mrs. K. Kubrick, late of rm 110, believed that Death was a terrible ordeal wherein one is ripped away from the bonds of this mortal coil. So, she was. It was the death she expected and so it was the death she got. She's resting quite comfortably now, somewhere in the tropics I understand. Most of the old folks go down south for eternity, warm weather and free brunch on the weekends."

"What about the backlog? Old folks don't have to wait?" Davis asked.

"As a general rule, no," Death answered. "They've waited enough in one lifetime; they should get a pass in the afterlife. In the case of clocking out, if...ah, your time runs out naturally, you get to go wherever it is you get to go. If you die, say by murder, before your time runs out then you have to wait around until your number gets called. Human beings, as you know, can be stupid nasty brutes who kill an awfully large number of their fellow stupid, nasty brutes. The waiting room is choked with people who died long before their time. That is the backlog. Some choose to keep themselves occupied and they all tend to end up in places like Winterbourne Home, where they can live fulfilling deaths until they are called. Others don't care to do anything more than wait and read very old magazines. They got rid of smoking down there a while ago. Let's say it wasn't accepted wholeheartedly at first."

"Wait, what?" Davis sputtered. "Are you telling me that nursing homes are populated by people that are already dead?"

"Not entirely," said Bob Newhart. "Some of them are employees. There are many living seniors in them but honestly, what better place to hide waiting dead people, than with people waiting to die? Changed the whole dynamic of those places for the better if you ask me. Why don't you ask me what you really want to know?"

"What about Jenn?" Davis asked without hesitation.

"She is a special case. She was killed long before her time was up, very long before, in fact. And her number was lost long ago when the offices moved from the top of a mountain in Greece to here. She doesn't exist in the system so she won't be sent anywhere. Not in the traditional sense anyway. I have offered to send her anywhere she wants to go after she fulfilled her role but she refused. She could be here until the end of time if she wanted."

Davis suddenly felt overwhelmingly grief-stricken for Jenn and wished she was here. He always felt better just having her around and now that he knew the truth about her, he felt as though he should try to return the favor and make her feel better about her situation.

"Has there ever been anyone else in her situation?" asked Davis.

"Only one other," said Bob Newhart. "The man who killed Jenn, I believe you already know him, was punished for what he did. Not because he killed her, which was bad enough in itself, but because he didn't prevent it. He was punished, some felt too harshly, for not doing the honorable, compassionate thing when he had the chance. He will walk the earth until..."

"Until when?" Davis asked.

"Until a Death comes forward and says he has paid enough. Until then, the Necrosites won't even answer his calls."

"He needs to pay for a very long time for what he did," Davis spat.

"Don't be so quick to judge, you saw what he left, what he lost? Some would say he suffered enough losing that. Remember, we are equal to all. We do not judge nor condemn."

Davis noticed that his face began to shimmer again but it wasn't just his face. His whole body began to flicker like a television signal in an electrical storm. Clear and bright one second, full of static and rolling the next.

"Aww crap," said Bob Newhart.

"What? What's happening?" Davis asked feeling a touch of panic.

"Something I...ah...hadn't planned on. Nancy Seasons has read the book and she is trying to trap me...ah...us"

He began to disappear. Flicker on and off and fade from view.

"Find Jenn," Death said. "And then find me."

CHAPTER 28

Davis ran out of the room and down the stone staircase. The steps seemed slicker now than they had been on the way up and he was afraid he might lose his footing and roll down the remaining stairs. He didn't relish the idea but reasoned if he did start to roll, as long as he didn't break his neck in the process, he would make it to the bottom of the stone stairs that much quicker. After he reached the bottom and stood in the glow of the orange closet light, he pushed open the wooden door and found himself back in Lois' room. She still lay in her bed and, so far as he could tell, she was still among the living.

"I'll be back, Lois. I promise," Davis said as he headed out of the room.

He ran to the nurse's station and stood in front of it for a moment, hoping Jenn would be there waiting for him, but she wasn't. Davis thought there would be nurses and residents wandering about—activity, the hustle and bustle of a nursing home in full swing— but there wasn't anything. It was as if time and life and the world had just come to a halt. Anxious to locate her, he ran down the hallways of his ward, glancing to the rooms, half expecting her to be wandering in and out of them visiting the residents as she often did. She wasn't to be found.

Davis didn't know why, but he sensed he did not have a great deal of time to stop Nancy Seasons from accomplishing what she planned to do and he knew if he didn't stop her, life, and death, as everyone knew it would never, ever, be the same.

The young man ran toward the double doors of the ward, not sure where he was going. He thought if he could find out where Nancy Seasons held Death, he could at least hold her off until Jenn arrived to tell him what to do. It was finding the room in time that proved to be a stumbling block. Davis pushed the right-hand door open and stopped dead when he caught sight of Jenn just out of the corner of his eye.

She stood behind the double doors of the unfinished hallway. Her face gray and worn out, as though she hadn't slept in many hours. But a smiled lit her face when she saw him. She waved him in to the other side of the door. When they were close enough, she embraced him and stepped back to look in his eyes. Davis noticed she was crying.

"I have to go find him," Davis said. "He just disappeared, Jenn, and I don't know where he is. He said I should find you and then go find him."

She pulled him close and he could feel her sobbing against his shoulder. The dark haired woman looked up at him again with tear stained eyes.

"I know," she said. "I know what he said and I know where he's been taken. I can take you there."

"Then why aren't we going?" Davis asked her.

Jenn viewed him apologetically and took his hands.

"Here's the thing," she began. "I can't go in there with you. Once we go to that room, I can't interfere or help you any further. Whatever you do must be done entirely of your own free will."

"Okay," said Davis. "Not a problem, so why are you crying?"

"My role in this life, the rundown of my clock was to find you. I found you and brought you here to him, to your destiny," She explained.

"And?" Davis asked. "I know about your lost number, Death told me all about it. I can help you go where you need to go."

"No," Jenn protested. "You don't understand. I don't want you to help me. I don't want to go anywhere, Davis, because I love you. I love you and I know what is waiting for you on the other side of that door and I can't do a single thing to help you."

Davis looked at her and let out a heavy sigh.

"It'll be okay," he said in false bravado.

"I will be all right with whatever decision you make," said Jenn. "But know this, if you show the slightest weakness, Nancy will kill you. Your soul, along with every living soul from now until forever, will suffer until someone more desperate comes along to take this terrible power away from her. And even that is no guarantee that you will be free from torment."

"Really?" Davis gasped.

"This is the real thing," Jenn replied. "If you walk away from all of it now, I will still love you, but none of us will come out of this unscathed."

"So I don't actually have a choice," Davis admitted.

"You do," said Jenn. "And it is a clear choice."

They walked hand in hand to the small white door and Davis paused before it.

"I can't do this, Jenn," he said. "I'm so scared."

"Think of Lois," Jenn said. "Think of the love you have for her and how you want her to meet her end. You will find strength in that."

She pulled him close and kissed him long.

"I'll be waiting here for you," she said.

Davis reached for the doorknob and the door swung, pulling away from his hand. He walked in and the door slammed behind him.

The pungent smell of blood nearly overwhelmed him as he walked forward into the small room. No small wonder, it was everywhere. The walls, what remained of them, were covered in bloody renderings of the symbols he had seen in the book, as was the floor. Ezra Schneider sat in a chair and, though there were no ropes or bonds of any kind holding him to it, he struggled to get up from it but remained firmly seated. His face was a bloody, pulpy mess. He looked as though he had been pummeled by someone or something much larger and stronger than he ever was. Davis walked to him and Ezra winked. The young man took it as a sign that in sprit, at least, Ezra was okay.

The room was now bathed, almost entirely, in the greasy blue light that was focused on the figures standing in the center of the room. There were two of them, one standing on a gigantic bloody symbol depicted on the floor, the other, visibly taller figure menaced above the smaller one. Davis recognized Bob Newhart as the smaller figure standing in the center of the blue light, his own blue eyes combined with the light streaming in through the walls, emitting a lurid glow. The other figure wasn't so much taller than Bob Newhart as it hovered above him and it resembled something that might have once been human. Its outer covering was the color of skin, though now scarcely visible through the bloody symbols that covered it and was stretched so impossibly thin, that it did little to cover the skeleton that was threatening to rupture up out of it with the slightest stressful movement. Its eyes were wide and staring, and glowed with the same greasy blue light that spilled into the room. The hair on its head was thin and stringy and blood soaked and may as well have been bits of old cord for all of the function it provided.

Davis stepped forward, moving toward him.

"Careful," warned the battered Ezra Schneider. "She's playing for keeps.

Davis understood that it was Nancy Seasons, or it had been once. He stood in front of Bob Newhart, attempting to shelter him from whatever this ruinous abomination had in store for him. Nancy eyed the young man as if he were a mosquito about to stick its nose in; she puffed out her sunken cheeks and blew a wisp of air that sent him flying toward the back of the room. Undeterred, he scrambled to his feet and walked to the center of the room again and stood in front of Death.

"Foolish thing," Nancy croaked. "How can you possibly hope to have the strength to fight for him, a stranger, when you hadn't the courage to fight for one you cared about? Look, she lies dying even now. I will be certain she spends eternity trapped in the withering corpse in her room as a reminder of your lack of conviction."

"You wouldn't dare," Davis hissed at the thing.

"Who would stop me?" Nancy said. "There is no time, you are out of TIME!"

"What?" Davis asked.

"Penlinio ger fy mron ac yn wynebu wedyn yn dod i ben!" she bellowed.

Both Davis and Bob Newhart fell to their knees and lifted their heads toward her as if powerless from the sound of her voice.

"Cyn bo hir byddwch yn mynd a'ch meistr gyda chi."

"The old words have no effect on this young man or me, you may cease using them."

"It is some kind of ancient magical language?" Davis asked.

"No," said Death. "It's Welsh. They figured it was going to end up a dead language because there were so few speakers left, so people started using it in rituals and that kind of thing, which in turn started a kind of revival of it. Boy, we didn't see that one coming."

"As you wish," Nancy said. "Now which one of you would like to go first?"

She didn't wait for an answer, instead she waved her hand and Bob Newhart began to rise. Now, completely surrounded by blue light, he began to shimmer. Not just his face, but all of his body. Like someone stood in front of him in the dark, turning a flashlight on and off so that one moment he was there and the next, he was gone. His face, while it appeared, looked clearly distressed.

"Stop it!" Davis shouted.

Nancy glided over to him and got face to face with him. "Why on earth would I stop?"

"It's me you want; I am the next one in line. His time is up. Let him go and you can have me."

It seemed to be a statement that got her attention and she went silent for a time, remaining completely motionless. She was so close to him, their noses almost touched. The Nancy thing's skin was shiny with perspiration and oily black ooze. Her nose seemed chewed away in spots and greasy blue eyes stared out malevolently from deep, sunken black sockets.

"I don't actually need to kill you anymore," she began, "my orderly long ago filled that role."

Davis could see the bloodied and twisted body of a large man dressed in white hospital scrubs.

"And your friend, Mr. Schneider, will prove an excellent blood sacrifice to finalize everything."

Davis looked around to Ezra who still struggled to free himself, had managed to get one arm loose and Davis started to think the old man would be free soon if he could just keep Nancy occupied long enough, but if it ended up toe to toe with her, how long could he hold out?

"But," she gurgled in a voice as perverse as it was gleeful, "I never did like you. I will kill you because I would like to do so, yes?"

"Sure," Davis said. "Why not?"

The young man wasn't certain how he would do it but knew keeping her attention firmly fixed on him was the best way for everyone concerned, to stay in the here and now.

She waved a hand and a bolt of greasy blue light flew from the cracks in the wall and caught him in the chest, knocking him flat on his back. He landed beside the huddled form of Death.

"Any suggestions?" Davis asked.

"You seem to be doing alright," Bob Newhart breathed.

She fired another blue bolt that exploded between the two of them. When Davis got back to his feet, he could see that Bob Newhart wasn't moving.

"No!" he shouted.

He bent down and grabbed Death's hand and felt nothing, no images, no heat. No life.

Davis turned to face Nancy as she bore down on him. He saw the greasy blue light brighten around him and he knew she was going to kill him this time, or worse, knock him out with it and take her time killing him. Either way, he didn't like his chances, so he held out a hand, like a traffic cop telling a car to stop on a street corner and to his surprise, Nancy stopped.

"What now?" Nancy wheezed. "I grow weary of these games."

"I would just like a chance to say goodbye," said Davis.

"To who?" asked Nancy.

"Whom," Corrected Ezra as he brought the chair down on top of the Nancy abomination's head, knocking her out cold.

"Go!" he said to Davis. "I don't imagine this is going to slow her down for long."

"Go where?" Davis asked frantically.

"I was hoping you knew," Ezra answered. "Look, just get the bastard hell out of here. Go somewhere that isn't here. I'll look after your friend. Just go!"

CHAPTER 29

D avis ran out of the room and didn't stop running until he cleared the double doors of the unfinished hallway. He knew he couldn't just run around Winterbourne forever, but if he could run long enough, the solution might present itself and so he stopped running.

"That's just about the dumbest thing I have ever thought."

He made it to the reception desk. Behind him the unfinished hallway beckoned and to his right the hallway to his ward stood empty. Directly in front of him, the exit. He could leave now. What would be the worst thing that would happen? He wasn't Death, he wasn't even a decent head cold. His hand felt the cold steel bar of the front door and he began to push.

"You can leave if you want." Jenn came around the reception desk. "Everything you believe in, not only in this place, but everywhere. Everything you have loved and lost, every memory you hold sacred will change, and soon it will all disappear. Once the balance shifts, it requires hundreds of years to put it right."

Davis lowered his head, afraid to look at her.

"I can't do it, Jenn," he finally admitted.

"You have something inside you that very few have. That is why you were picked. Whether you accept the gift is entirely up to you."

"But he's gone, Nancy has already won. I felt his hand and got nothing, it was ice cold."

"Um...he's Death, the Servant of the Void, the..."

"Yeah, I got that. What's your point?"

"He's dead, Jim. The only way Nancy can truly win anything is by you refusing to take his place."

"Isn't there supposed to be a ceremony or something?" Davis asked.

"Words were spoken in Welsh the night you were born and the robe and scythe were set aside until the time came for you to make your choice. That time is now."

She walked to him, reached up and kissed his lips.

"I will love you no matter what you choose," Jenn said and walked toward the unfinished hallway. Davis watched her open the doors, thinking she would look back at him. She walked through the double doors and disappeared into the blackness of the hallway.

He thought about Lois. Nancy would have the Necrosites rip her apart just enough to suffer but not to send her on her way. She would likely keep Ezra as a plaything, tormenting him whenever the mood struck her. And what about Jenn? What would that awful crone do to Jenn when she found out the woman he loved was Limbo's only permanent resident?

He walked silently toward the doors of his ward and looked through the double windows to the nurse's station, where it was dark and still. *Where were all the people?* Davis wondered. It was as if someone had scooped everyone up and hidden them away somewhere, the place was deserted. He pushed the door open and crouched down, feeling a little foolish after he realized that no one was coming to attack so he stood up and slowly walked in.

Davis passed the nurse's station and saw it was full of Necrosites, some sitting at the computers wearing nurse's hats and others standing on the desk staring at him through the big bay window. They watched him suspiciously but did not follow. He held his breath as he passed the station, thinking they would burst out at any minute and have at him but they remained cautiously still as the young man rounded the corner to the hallway that led to Lois' room.

Mareth could see thin beams of greasy blue light coming out of the door frames of every room and a thin pale mist hovered above the floor. At least 15 Necrosites milled around Lois' door, as though standing guard or waiting for someone to tell them to clear off. Davis took a deep breath and headed for the door, he made a rush for the biggest of them figuring if he got one good shot in and knocked him down, the other ones might just back away from him. As he closed the distance, Nancy Seasons burst through the door and knocked him back against the wall. She fired off a quick burst of blue light from between her hands and Davis rolled away just as a shower of glass and wood rained down beside him.

"I told you, boy," she hissed, "you were too late. Now I have become Death, destroyer of worlds."

Nancy drew in a large breath and let loose another blast of blue.

Davis pushed himself up and flew at her. His fist connected with the skeletal face. He felt teeth dislodge as he began to rain blows on it. One fist after another. He continued to bash Nancy's face until he was certain she was no longer moving. He stood over her. Nudged her. When she remained still, he moved away and headed for the door to Lois' room. He expected the Necrosites to stop him but the largest of the group stepped in front of him and spoke.

"We have sworn loyalty of the True Servant of the Void. You are not that servant."

"Then I am too late," replied Davis.

"This creature is not that servant either," the Necrosite said. "Death is the shepherd of souls. It is not enough to merely kill; it is also for the Servant of the Void to free the spirit."

The big Necrosite stood aside and let Davis pass.

He entered the room to find Lois still unconscious on the bed. The young man walked to her and took hold of her hand. Her eyes opened slowly.

"Jimmy," she whispered. "I was hoping to see you again."

"I'm right here Lois."

"I know," she said. "You've always been here."

He felt his eyes begin to well up as she squeezed his hand.

"I'm so tired, Jimmy," Lois said.

"Go to sleep then Lois." Davis brushed her cheek with the back of his hand. He knew she wasn't talking about sleep but neither was he. His friend had become old, frail, and afraid and she didn't have the strength to fight anymore.

"I can't, Jimmy." She closed her eyes and turned away.

Ezra Schneider and Bob Newhart rounded the corner, heading for Lois' room just as Nancy started to rise. Bob Newhart rushed toward her and stood in the middle of the Necrosites.

"Gweinwch eich gwir meistr ac ymosod arni," said Death.

The Necrosites set on Nancy, ripping and tearing at her paper thin flesh.

"That's only going to buy us a little time," he said.

"I thought you were powerless now?" Ezra asked.

"There's a little Death in these old hands yet," Bob Newhart said. "It still has a few privileges."

"I need to see how he's doing," said Death.

"I'll hold ass balls off, not like she can kill me, right?"

"If that makes you feel better, you go ahead and think that."
Ezra smiled at him.

"Well, then it's been a bastard of a good run."

"It has," Death smiled.

Davis flung himself up from Lois' bed as he heard the door open.

He stood stunned when he saw what came in through the door. It wasn't Nancy, or the Necrosites, but the small black-winged boy.

"I don't know what to do," Davis said.

"You have always known what to do," said the boy. "Let your heart guide your hand and let your friend go."

Davis stood trembling, knowing what it meant and still so very frightened of it all. He bent over Lois lying prostrate on the bed and kissed her forehead.

"I will miss you Lois, sleep now."

With trembling hands, he held two fingers out above her head, feeling slightly foolish and terribly disconsolate at what was going to happen next. He rubbed the two fingers across her head from one side to the other and kissed her forehead again. A wave of contentment washed over him. The small black-winged boy walked up to him and repeated the gesture, rubbing two fingers from one side of his forehead to the other and kissing him gently. Davis felt a tremendous surge of heat filter through his body, starting at the tops of his toes and moving up past his legs into his chest, finally flowing out of the top of his head. It was over as quickly as it began and Davis was now aware he was cold. Colder than he had ever been in his life, as though he might never be warm again.

"You are now the True Servant of the Void, use this gift well and maintain the balance lest the world fall."

"What about Nancy?" Davis asked.

"She has no more power over you. She, like all others, must kneel before the great leveler. You may do with her as you will."

"Who are you?" Davis asked the boy.

"I am The Omega, I am The Void."

Davis glanced at Lois lying on the bed and saw the look of tranquility on her face. Whatever misgivings he had about taking on the mantle of the Grim Reaper, they all disappeared as he gazed into her face.

He turned around to see the boy gone and Bob Newhart standing in his place.

"What do I do now?" asked Davis.

"Meet me back upstairs in about an hour and I'll go through everything with you," said Death. "You'll want to take out the trash before you come up."

"The trash?" Davis asked, confused by the statement.

"I believe she is playing with Ezra right now. She is still dangerous, like a cornered animal. Don't let your guard down. She can't hurt you but could do harm to the people around you."

"I have something special in mind for her," Davis said.

"I thought you might." Bob Newhart disappeared into the closet.

Davis stepped outside the room to stand in the doorway. He saw Ezra struggling to hold onto a weakened but still very lethal Nancy Seasons. She had regained much of her former appearance, though her hair remained stringy and matted and though they were fading and slowly returning to their former mud brown color, her eyes were still the same color as Davis'.

"Don't come any closer," Ezra said to him. "Ass balls here still packs a bastarding good wallop."

He stepped out of the doorway and the Necrosites immediately looked to him and bent down on one knee. As best as they could anyway, Necrosites are far too low to the ground in the first place to kneel. It was less like kneeling and more like spastic lurching followed by falling over but the effect was not lost on Davis.

"Stand up my friends," he said to them.

"What will you have us do, my Lord?" asked the big Necrosite.

"Stand back," Davis said.

He looked to Nancy Seasons and told Ezra to let go of her.

"Are you sure about this?" Ezra asked.

"Let her go," Davis said again, "and move away."

Ezra released his grip on Nancy and moved next to the Necrosites, figuring he was safer with them somehow. He readied himself to leap on her at a moment's notice.

"You assholes ready?" he asked the Necrosites who growled at him then turned to face Nancy Seasons with claws and teeth at the ready.

Nancy Seasons stood up and clenched her hands into tight pudgy fists. Streaks of blue light and sparks erupted from them and she turned to face Davis.

"That is the last mistake you will ever make, yes?"

She opened her hands and held them slightly apart. A ball of blue light and sparks began to build between them. It grew to the size of a basketball, sizzling and popping as it expanded and a cancerous smile stretched across her face. Her eyes narrowed and she hurled the ball toward him.

CHAPTER 30

Davis Mareth watched the ball of blue sparks hurtle toward him and braced for the impact, but it didn't come. Instead, it passed through him with a sound like a feather passing through a cloud. He walked to Nancy and took hold of her wrists. She tried to wrestle away from him.

"You get your obscene hands off of me Mr. Mareth, do you hear me?" Nancy screeched. "You can consider your employment here at Winterbourne at an end. Do you hear what I'm saying to you?"

She forcibly jerked her wrist, tried to break away from his gentle but vice-like grip.

"You let go of me right fucking now!" There was terror rising in the southern accent that lay deep beneath her voice as he took hold of one of her hands.

He got a flash of a chubby little girl, sitting alone pulling the wings off of flies and watching them writhe around in agony. Davis flashed again and saw a chubby high school girl, tormenting a scrawny, weak-willed girl with glasses, lying on the floor of a gym locker room. He saw the first person she had ever trussed up and terrified to death, all the way down to the death of the orderly a few hours ago, all the while looking for the sad little girl behind it, or the terrible secret she never told anyone that had turned her into this twisted and black soul. If it was in there at all, it was buried so deep inside of her that even he couldn't find it. He suspected there never had been such a wounded child inside her and she was just willful and bully enough to push her way through life and become the unchallenged, evil piece of work she had grown into. The new Death kissed her gently and rubbed her forehead from one side to the other.

"Goodbye, Nancy," Davis said.

Nancy Seasons' eyes closed as she sunk slowly to the floor, like a balloon with a slow leak.

"Rydych yn gwybod wahat i dowith hi," Davis said and the Necrosites took Nancy and walked into Lois' empty room.

"Where are they taking her?" Ezra asked.

"No idea," said Davis. "That's why I said they would know what to do with her. Somewhere warm with a nice breeze, I hope."

He turned to Ezra, a man he was fully prepared to write off as a murderer only a few hours ago. Now left speechless by the man he owed his life to.

"Ezra, I…"

"You don't have to say anything kid. I did a terrible thing a very long time ago. I thought I was doing it for the right reason and I was punished for my lack of bravery."

"Come with me," Davis said to him.

The two walked back to the nurse's station and Davis found a small piece of paper. He opened closed drawers and cupboards with frantic abandon.

"You'd think in a place where there was so much bloody paperwork, you could find a goddamned pen."

Ezra reached into the left inside pocket of his jacket and produced a blue pen.

Davis took the pen and began to write on the small piece of paper. He looked up and smiled after he finished writing and handed it to Ezra.

"When you get to where you're going, give them this."

He took hold of Ezra's hand and shook like he was wishing a safe journey to an old friend about to board a plane. The younger man leaned into him and Ezra pulled away with a sudden jerk.

"I will knock out your bastarding teeth if you try to kiss me."

"Fair enough." Davis took two fingers and rubbed them from one side of Ezra's forehead to the other then held him behind the shoulders and eased his friend to the ground.

"Say hi to your little girl for me."

He walked back into Lois' room and headed for the closet. There was no light coming from it but the steps were there all the same. He was amazed at how easily he could traverse them now. The stairs still felt wet and slippery under his feet but he seemed to be able to grip them now, as if his feet had grown claws. "Stanger things have happened."

When he reached the top of the stairs he could see Bob Newhart standing beside the big oak desk, wearing Bermuda shorts and an Acapulco shirt frantically staring at his watch.

"Oh good, you're here."

"I had a few things to take care of," said Davis.

"Oh," said Death. "So, I ah, I suppose you thought it was okay for you to just, ah, go ahead and do all of your stuff and not worry about what anybody else had to do today?"

"Sorry," said Davis. "I didn't figure you were doing anything."

"I have a plane to catch and a retirement to begin," said Bob Newhart.

"But don't you…die now?" Davis asked.

"No," said Death. "How old would you say I am?"

"You look to be about 75," said Davis.

"I was 15 when I accepted the scythe and robe. That is 60 years of living I have to do before I die. Not doing anything? My boy, I am going to do *everything*."

"But weren't you going to tell me all about this job, what I had to do?"

"It's all in the big book on the desk," said Bob Newhart. "If you have any questions, you can ask your new secretary."

She put a hand on his shoulders and he jumped at the unexpected contact.

"She comes with the office," said Death. "Her paperwork got lost a long time ago, you can send her on her way if you'd like. She has been around an awfully long time."

Bob Newhart picked up a battered Gladstone bag and headed toward the staircase.

"See you in 60 years," he said and descended the staircase.

Davis turned to Jenn.

"Now Ms. Henderson, I run a tight ship here, I am tough but I am fair and I think you will find that I…"

She grabbed him and covered his face in kisses. Every time he tried to break away and finished talking she pulled him tighter and kissed him more.

"We've got a lot of work to do," Davis said.

"You're right," Jenn said and continued to kiss him.

"I'm serious!" he protested.

"So am I," she continued.

When she finally let him up for air, Jenn looked to Davis, "What happened to Ezra?"

"Let's say he got what he deserved," Davis said.

"And Nancy?"

"She wanted to be around forever and now she will."

Jenn looked at him with confusion and a slightly bewildered smile.

EPILOGE

Nancy Seasons stood midway in a line up, uncertain what she was there for.

"What are we waiting for?" she asked the man ahead of her.

"This is the line to get your number," said the man.

"A number to get seen by a demise agent. You don't get seen by one of them, you don't go anywhere for eternity and then you're stuck in this waiting room."

Nancy looked ahead of them and saw there were thousands of people waiting in line. Behind her was even worse. "I'm not standing in this line, yes? Don't they know who I am?"

She started to leave the line and the man ahead of her spoke.

"You'll lose your place and have to go to the end of the line."

She looked behind her again and stepped quietly back behind the man. Nancy lowered her head and tried not to think about spending the next hundred years or so standing in this line. A commotion and she looked to see where it was coming from but could only hear raised voices.

"Get your bastarding hands off me!"

Nancy smiled. At least she would get where she was going before Ezra Schneider and that sweetened the sting of this line just a little.

A Necrosite came over to Ezra and demanded to know why he was not in line. Ezra dug in the pocket of his jacket and produced the note Davis had given him which read,

This man has suffered and redeemed himself more than any
I have ever known. See to it that he gets to his destination
quickly. Treat him with the upmost respect.

Signed D.

The Necrosite grunted and took Ezra's hand. They began to walk to the big desk at the front of the room. Ezra caught Nancy's eye as he passed her.

"See you on the other side, yes?"

Ezra Schneider smiled and let the Necrosite lead him to the big desk. He could smell his daughter's hair in the breeze and hear her laughter in the rumble of the crowd and knew he was going home.

The End

S. A. Baker is a healthcare worker and recovering professional musician who spent eleven years touring around North America and despite popular opinion, he really does know how to smile.

From early on, he excelled at telling stories and won several local writing awards before being bitten by the rock and roll bug.

He currently lives in a small town in Ontario with his wife and two children and two of the dumbest cats that have ever drawn breath. When not writing, Mr. Baker plays bagpipes competitively (no, really) and thinks about learning to fly fish. Winterbourne is S. A. Baker's first novel and is the introductory story in the Winterbourne saga.